A Promise to Love

A Promise
to Love

Lorraine E. Thomas

First Printing June 2009

ISBN 978-0-9824006-9-2
Library of Congress Control Number: 2009929331

Published by: His Word In Season Publishing

Post Office Box 801479
Acworth, GA 30101
www.hiswordinseason.com

Scripture quotations are from THE NEW KING JAMES VERSION ® of the Bible. Copyright © 1982 by Thomas Nelson, Inc.

Printed in the United States of America

Cover Design: Tamara Finkbeiner
Edited by: E. Swalberg and C. Thomas

To my family and friends,

I appreciate your encouragement and support.

There is no fear in love.

1 John 4:18a (NKJV)

❧ *Chapter 1* ❦

It was hard to keep from smiling as I looked down at the paper in my hand. Finally, things were looking up for me.

"Did you miss me?" The familiar voice sent chills down my spine. I turned slowly toward my husband. The words that he had spoken to me only weeks before raced through my mind.

"It's never going to be over!"

Where are my keys? My hands shook violently trying to find the car keys that I had carelessly thrown into my purse earlier. Rodney came up behind me and caressed my arm as he embraced me. It was too late to try to escape. My body stiffened and my heart raced wildly. *God, please help me,* I prayed silently. Why did he have to show up now when everything was just starting to turn around for me?

Rodney turned me around to face him. "You seem surprised to see me and you didn't answer my question, "Did you miss me?" He held my face tightly and waited for my response.

I was too shocked and frightened to do or say anything. He loosened his grip and smiled.

"When did you get here?" I stammered weakly.

"Yesterday," he said as his eyes held mine.

Yesterday! Had he followed me to school today? "So how did you know I was here?" I asked innocently.

Rodney smiled and looked down at the paper that I still clutched nervously. He took the paper from my hand and looked at the grade on my test. "You got an A+. You must have been doing a lot of studying," he said snidely.

The joy I'd experienced only moments before over my first A since entering college slowly seeped out of me as he looked at the paper scornfully.

"Did Mama tell you where I was?" I asked again.

Rodney looked up at me slowly. "No, I saw you leave the house this morning. I wanted to make sure you weren't going to meet your man, so I followed you." He watched me closely for a reaction.

I tried to pull away from him, but he pulled me closer. "You're hurting me," I said, trying to pull away from him again. He loosened his grip and pulled my face toward him. The liquor on his breath was strong. He continued to pull me in closer.

"I don't know what it's going to take to get through to you Dee-Dee, but you're my wife and I'm not letting you go. Do I make myself clear?"

The tears began to roll down my cheek as I nodded. He let go of my face and stood there looking at me. "Now, we've been through a lot, but that's normal. All new couples have problems."

I brushed the tears from my cheeks angrily. "So what happens now?"

Rodney frowned. "What do you mean what happens now? You are coming back with me."

"No! I'm in college," I cried hysterically. "I am not quitting school Rodney. We still have some things we need to work through and I'm not…"

Rodney snatched my arm and held it tight. "We'll just see about that!" He pulled my arms up behind me and started pushing me toward a grey car.

"No," I screamed and pushed his arms away.

"Dee-Dee, wake up. You dreamin' baby."

I tried to push away the hand that was shaking me.

"Come on, Baby. Wake up."

My eyes flew open. It took me a few minutes to get myself together as my mother held me.

"It's OK. It was just a bad dream," Mama said as she brushed my hair away from my face.

"But it seemed so real."

Mama chuckled. "That must a been some dream. You were six years old the last time I had to wake you up after a bad dream." She propped my pillows up behind me.

"Sorry Mama."

"No need to be sorry. So what was the dream about?"

"I dreamed that Rodney was after me and I couldn't get away from him. It was silly Mama. I'm sorry you had to come all the way up here."

Mama patted my hand as she got up from the bed. "I was on my way to Pearl's house when I heard you up here screamin'. Somethin' triggered the dream?"

"I was talking to Francine about him before I dozed off."

Mama nodded. "It's good you tryin' to get some rest. I hear you movin' around in here in the middle of the night. Why don't you come on over to Pearl's when you get yosef together. We got a bushel of oysters."

I thought about the offer and nodded. It might do me some good to get out of here for awhile. "I'll come over later."

"You need anything before I go?"

I shook my head. She looked at me sadly before hobbling to the door.

Mama closed the door quietly. Her feet were badly swollen and she was having a very hard time going up and down the stairs. I sighed loudly and squeezed my eyes shut. I was shaken by the dream and sat there for several minutes trying to force it from my mind.

Last night had been a good night for me. It was the first night since coming back home, that I hadn't cried myself to sleep. Being here with Mama was exactly what I needed right now, but it was difficult trying to talk to her about my life in Tennessee. The mere mention of Rodney's name made her clench her fists tightly. It was clear that she was afraid for me. She checked the locks on the doors repeatedly before going to bed and often made me promise not to go anywhere by myself. She felt that Rodney would try to hurt me if he got me alone somewhere, so she did everything in her power to keep me close. That wasn't such a hard thing to do these days. There was no place for me to go.

None of this would be happening if I had just listened to Mama when she begged me not to marry Rodney in the first place. She saw the signs that I had refused to acknowledge back then. Never in my wildest dreams did I think it would end this way.

Why had I been so stubborn? It was in this very room that I had conspired how to get Mama to agree to let me marry Rodney. Many of the things she said were true. She told me that my decision to give up my dream of going to nursing school in order to marry right out of high school was too hasty. I'd allowed Rodney to manipulate and control me from the very beginning. Now we were both paying the price for that decision and it was causing my mother a lot of stress. It was pointless to try to keep Mama from worrying about me. She worried every time I walked out the door to go job hunting, but getting a job was my first priority.

"You should give yosef time to rest Dee-Dee."

"I know Mama, but I need a job. You can't keep giving me money. Besides, I wouldn't be in this mess if I had listened to you."

I had to admit that it was scary going out and not knowing when or where Rodney would show up, but I couldn't spend the rest of my life in the house. I tried to be careful, but there was no way for me to know if Rodney was in town. He was furious that I had gone to his commander and the local police about the abuse and there was no doubt that he would try to get even.

Half an hour later, I joined Mama at Ms. Pearl's house. The house was hot and muggy so I decided to sit on the porch after being there for only a few minutes. The July afternoon was stifling, but I didn't want to sit in the house with Mama and her two friends. I cared about them deeply and knew that they only wanted what was best for me, but I didn't want to answer any more questions about my estranged husband.

I swatted lamely at a pesky mosquito that kept buzzing around my ear. After awhile, a cool breeze began to blow. Hopefully, it would bring an end to the humid temperatures. It was hard to ignore the faint sound of the ocean waves as they lapped gently at the shore. I took a deep breath. There was no mistaking the perfume of honeysuckle that mingled with the musky odor of the salt water. *A rain shower would be nice right now.*

Summers in South Carolina were extremely hot. Thankfully, Mama's house was close to the ocean. As a teen, my friends and I used to enjoy going to the water's edge to splash around for a bit to cool off.

"Dee-Dee, you sure you don't want some of these oysters?" Mama called from the kitchen. I squinted to see through the screen door and looked at the women as they shucked oysters and quickly plopped them into their mouths. Ms. Pearl and Ms. Lucille motioned for me to come in and join them. They had decided this morning to use Ms. Pearl's back porch for the oyster roast since they had used Mama's house the last time.

"They nice and plump," Mama said as she drenched another plump oyster in hot sauce.

Ms. Lucille nodded her head quickly before smacking her lips. "I sure hope we have enough left to make the stew."

"Yeah, we need a handful to fry for breakfast too," Ms. Pearl chuckled.

"At the rate we going, we won't have none left," Mama said without waiting for my answer.

I turned back to the sound of the Atlantic tide slapping against the wood at the edge of the landing. My thoughts returned to Rodney. It had taken him almost two weeks before he finally had the chance to talk to me. Mama always managed to intercept his calls and hung up on him as soon as she recognized his voice. Last Friday was the first time that he had gotten through to me after I snatched the phone up quickly thinking that it was one of the counselors from the university. I had registered for the fall semester the week after returning home to Mama, hoping that it wouldn't be too late to get in. But it wasn't the call I'd been waiting for. The angry snarl on the other end startled me.

"So you think you got one over on me huh?" Even though he was miles away, I stood speechless with the phone clenched tightly in my hand.

"You think you can try to ruin my career and get away with it," he snapped furiously.

Every ounce of my being wanted to hang up the phone, but I stood rooted to the spot.

"Because of your lies about me, you caused me to lose my PFC rank and get busted down to a private. You may think it's over, but it's not!"

If Rodney were standing in front of me, there was no doubt that he would have his hands around my throat. I shivered at the thought and suddenly found my voice. "You deserved whatever you got Rodney. You had no right to put your hands on me!"

"You are my wife," he yelled into the phone.

I held the phone away from my ear as he continued to rant and rave. I hung up the phone. What a mess! It was hard to block his angry words from my mind and now it was causing me to have bad dreams. I groaned softly and made circles in the soft white sand with my toes.

It would be nice to talk to Francine right now. I missed her. She had been such a good friend to me in Tennessee. Things used to be that way with Cynthia and me, but our relationship was not the same. We had grown apart even though we had been best friends since grade school. So much had changed in our lives. There was no way that I could ever tell her what had happened to me in Tennessee. I called her a couple days after coming home. She came to see me a few times, but things weren't the same as before.

I wasn't the carefree young woman who used to enjoy the late night parties. Cynthia must have sensed that there was something going on between Rodney and me. She asked about him a few times, but I made sure that the conversations ended quickly. It would have been too embarrassing to tell her the truth, so I told her that Rodney was away on a long field problem and we thought it best for me to come home to be with Mama for a while. Thankfully, she didn't keep pressing me for more information.

Francine on the other hand was like the sister I never had. "Just remember that the rest of your life is still ahead of you," she had said the last time we talked. We could talk freely about everything except Walter. The thought of what I had done to him made me cringe. He did not deserve to be treated that way. I knew that he had feelings for me and it was wrong to lead him on. I was hesitant to ask Francine about him for fear that she would think that I was still interested in him.

"So how are things at church?" It was a question that I hoped would encourage her to volunteer some information about him.

"Things are good. We are having our Family Fun Day on Saturday. I'm in charge of the cake walk. Can you imagine that? She laughed before adding, "Guess who will be in the dunking booth?"

"Don't tell me you are volunteering to do that too," I laughed.

"No not me, Walter." Francine chuckled softly. "Girl, I sure wish you could be here, but I know that's out of the question."

"Yeah, I wish I could be there too. So how is Walter doing? Has he found a wife yet, I asked playfully." My heart began to race wildly as I waited for her answer.

"A wife, are you kidding me?" Francine said incredulously. "I doubt that Walter will be looking for a wife anytime soon."

I silently prayed that it wasn't because of me that he now felt that way.

"I didn't mean to suggest that you…"

"I know what you mean," I replied. "I can't say that I would blame him. Has he talked to you at all about what happened?"

Francine sighed softly.

"You don't have to tell me if you don't want to," I added quickly hoping that she would tell me anyway.

"No, it's not that. It's just that I feel so bad for him sometimes. He's always asking if I heard from you and wants to know how you're doing. I shouldn't be telling you this Claudette. I know that you had feelings for him too, even though you never came out and said it."

I didn't trust myself to answer.

"He is concerned that your husband may try to hurt you. I guess he just wants to make sure that you have a way to protect yourself. By the way, have you heard anymore about what the Army did to your husband for his affair with Teresa?"

"No, I got in touch with Sergeant Ramirez to see what was going on. They gave him an Article 15, which is a bad report on his record and took a rank from him. She said he was also confined to the barracks for a few months and they moved Teresa Collins to a new unit."

"Is that all that happened to her?"

"Sergeant Ramirez said she didn't want to divulge any additional information about Collins that didn't directly pertain to Rodney. So I assume something else happened to her, but she couldn't tell me."

"She deserved whatever she got," Francine said adamantly. "Both of them did! They knew what they were doing. I wish they could have been hog-tied together and whipped!"

I laughed loudly at Francine and shook my head. "Girl you are crazy," but I agree that they should have been punished. "I'm just glad it's over."

"Is it?"

Francine's question caught me by surprise. "What do you mean?"

"Is it really over for you? You haven't really talked to him since all of this happened. How is it all going to be resolved? Do you even know what you want to do?"

It was hard to answer her question because I wasn't quite sure what I wanted to do. "I guess I don't really know what I want at this point," I said sadly.

"You need to start thinking about it Claudette. The rest of your life is still ahead of you."

"Yeah, I know. It's just so hard right now."

We were both silent for a moment.

"Well, you take care of yourself. I gotta go."

"I'll talk to you later."

Francine's words ran through my mind when Rodney called the next day, so I decided to take his call. She was right. The problem was not going to go away. I had to come to a decision about Rodney. At first, he seemed shocked that I had decided to talk to him after hanging up on him several times before.

"You ready to head on back home Dee-Dee," Mama asked. Her voice startled me. I had been lost in my own little world as I thought about the events of the past few weeks.

"I packed some oysters for you to eat later in case you get hungry." Mama yawned as she stood beside me on the porch.

I quickly jumped up and brushed off the back of my pants. Ms. Pearl and Ms. Lucille soon followed her onto the porch.

"Well I gotta go before it gets too dark out here for me to see. I don't need to be pickin' myself up off the ground," Ms. Lucille said as she slowly made her way down the steps.

"Dee-Dee can see you home Lucille. You know you blind as a bat at night."

"And who is gonna see you home? I can see better than you. Remember, I'm only a few months older than you," Ms. Lucille said playfully.

We all laughed as we turned to go home. I could hear Ms. Pearl chuckling behind us as we walked across the street.

❧ *Chapter 2* ❧

*I*t had been another restless night of tossing and turning. *I might as well get up.* There was no way that I was going to be able to go back to sleep now. The many recurring bad dreams were causing me to have sleepless nights. I clutched my robe around me tightly and walked gingerly down the steps to keep from waking Mama. It would be another hour or so before she got up. She was sure to fix a big breakfast of homemade biscuits, ham, eggs scrambled with cheese, and whatever else she had a taste for.

After filling the tea kettle with water, I looked around our tiny kitchen. It was here that I had convinced Mama to let me marry Rodney. I was standing in this very spot when I told Mama that Rodney would never hurt me. *Boy was I wrong.*

Mama's words came rushing back to me. "Everything he learned 'bout being a man, he learned from his daddy; Can the son be any different?"

I groaned. *What am I going to do?* I still loved Rodney, but things would have to be different this time if we were going to be together. Unfortunately, he didn't think there was anything wrong. He kept telling me that I needed to be more like his mother. Rodney's mother felt that I was wrong for leaving my husband.

"The Good Book says, 'wives are to submit to their husband'," she often said to me.

I shook my head and thought about the months that I had lived with my mother-in-law when Rodney went away to Boot Camp. There was no doubt that the woman was deathly afraid of her husband after suffering through many of his beatings. He was rarely at home and I couldn't remember ever hearing him say a kind word to her. *Why in the world would anybody want to live that way?*

A few minutes later, I heard Mama's heavy steps coming downstairs. "What you doin' up so early," she said and she shuffled into the kitchen. Mama grimaced as she sat down in her favorite chair. The chair creaked loudly as she settled in. "Somethin' wrong Baby?"

The tea kettle whistled behind me. I quickly reached over to turn the stove off before reaching for my cup. "You want some tea Mama?" I glanced at her in time to see her shake her head slowly.

"No Baby. I need a minute to get myself together. I ate too many of those oysters yesterday. My pressure might be a little high. Now what's wid the long face?"

I sighed deeply. "I was just thinking about my marriage to Rodney that's all."

Mama frowned and began to rub her knees. She seemed to be in deep thought. She only rubbed her knees like that when her arthritis was acting up. She often joked about needing to get oiled up first before things would start working right.

"I know you still love him Dee-Dee, even after all you been through. I can't tell you what to do. He is your husband and this is your life. I do know that it's not right for a man to be hittin' on a woman like he doin'. You only got one life to live and no woman should have to go through life bein' beat up all the time."

I stirred the tea bag around in the hot water and walked over to the table. The hot steam swirled into my face as I took a quick sip before sitting down. "You're right."

"I was married to Earl Chapman for near forty years and he never raised a hand to hit me. God bless his soul. That ain't to say we didn't have problems. Every couple go through problems, but a man beatin' up on his wife not the way to solve it. Just make sure you pray before you make a decision. God won't lead you wrong."

I nodded to show Mama that I understood what she was saying. "It's still hard to believe that things turned out the way it did. I just didn't think that Rodney could ever be like his father."

"Baby, the apple don't fall far from the tree. The best way to find out how a man gonna treat you is to see how his daddy treat his mama. A man can't do no better if he don't know no better. You still love him, but it'll be better to love him from a distance than to go back to him and let him kill you." Mama rubbed her knees again and eased herself up out of the chair.

Was the stress of all of this causing her arthritis to act up so bad? It saddened me to know that my situation with Rodney could be causing Mama so much pain. She walked over the sink. The phone rang as soon as she reached the counter. We both stared at it, surprised that someone would be calling this early in the morning.

Mama reached over and picked it up before it could ring a third time. "Hello." She held the phone to her chest before turning to look at me. "Now is a good a time as any to let him know how things stand. I'm going to sit out on the porch for a little bit and let the sun warm up these old bones." She pushed the phone toward me.

My heart sank as I took the phone from her and braced myself for the angry words that awaited me. Mama shuffled toward the front door.

"Hello." I answered curtly.

"Hey, it's me. I didn't mean what I said the other day on the phone."

I held the phone tightly to my ear surprised that Rodney had called to apologize to me. This was new for him.

"Well. Aren't you going to say something?"

I twisted the phone cord around my fingers as I searched for the right words. "I heard you. I just don't know what to say right now."

"Look, I know we are going through a lot right now, but we can work things out."

"How are we going to do that when you think that you can hit me whenever you want and see nothing wrong with it!" I could feel myself getting angry all over again.

"You are my wife!"

"And what does that mean, Rodney? Does that mean that I'm your punching bag?"

"See, I knew you would start in on that again. Why you gotta keep bringing up the past? All that's over! Look, I didn't call to argue with you."

I was fuming at this point. "So you think we should just go on like nothin' happened?"

"That's what couples do. You don't just run back home when things get hard. You work them out."

"Well, I think that we need some time apart. I've enrolled in school and I'm going back to get my degree in…" I jumped when I heard a loud thump on the other end.

"Dee-Dee as soon as I get off restriction and save up enough money to get another car, I'm coming to get you. Your place is here with me and that's all there is to it!"

I took a deep breath. "I think we need some time apart. You…"

"I don't care what you think. I'm the man and you do what I say. I know you got your mama down there filling your head…"

I snatched the phone away from my ear and hung up. I stood there staring at it angrily. The phone rang again and I immediately picked it up and yelled into the receiver. "We don't have anything else to talk about Rodney." I slammed the phone down again and turned to go upstairs. By this time Mama had walked back into the house to see what was going on. We both looked at the phone when it rang again. Mama walked over to the phone in the living room and snatched it off the hook.

"Yes!" She frowned as she listened to the voice on the other end. "Now you listen to me, Dee-Dee done told you she don't want to talk to you right now, so don't call here again today!" Mama slammed the phone down and stood there daring it to ring again.

I held my breath praying that Rodney wouldn't be stupid enough to call back. After a few seconds went by without the phone ringing, she took a deep breath and went into the kitchen.

"If he calls again, don't you answer, I'll get it."

I nodded, sorry that Mama had to get involved in our argument.

"I'm gettin' ready to fix some breakfast. You hungry," Mama said tightly.

I shook my head. I knew that it would be difficult to eat anything right now. "No thanks. I'm going up to my room for awhile." I could feel Mama watching me as I headed back upstairs. I plopped down on my bed and let the pent up emotions break free. It didn't seem possible that things would work out with Rodney and me. He was too pig-headed to listen to anything I had to say. His words played over and over again in my head. "When I get off restriction and save up enough money to get another car…"

What had happened to his car? Surely the army hadn't taken his car away from him too. *Can they do that*, I wondered. But why would he need another car? Maybe he wrecked the other one. I sat there trying to figure out why he had said that as the savory smell of the hickory smoked bacon tickled my nose. My stomach growled loudly. *Maybe I'm hungrier than I thought.*

I found Mama sitting at the kitchen table just about to say grace over her food. She looked up as I walked into the kitchen. "I made extra if you hungry. Go fix yourself a plate."

It amazed me how Mama always seemed to know what I needed.

"Thanks Mama. I think the hunger pains got the best of me."

She smiled as she buttered her biscuit. "Get me the honey out of the cabinet would you, she said sheepishly. I need to leave all that sugar alone, but I just want to drizzle a little bit on this biscuit."

I laughed as I reached into the cabinet and found the small jar of honey. I handed it to her and tried to keep my mouth from watering as I quickly filled my plate with the buttery grits and sausage. I sat next down next to her and quickly prayed over my food. I had eaten half of what was on my plate before looking up at Mama. She was eyeing me as she sipped her coffee.

"Did you make up your mind about something that he didn't agree to," she asked before putting her cup down.

I put my fork down and thought about what I had said to make him so angry. "He doesn't want me going to school. He says as soon as he gets off restriction and has enough money to get another car, he's coming to get me." I waited for her response.

Mama sat there frowning as she chewed a piece of bacon slowly. "What happened to his car?"

I shrugged. "Maybe he wrecked it."

"So, he says he comin' to get you. What if he just shows up one day Dee-Dee?" Mama's voice trembled and I knew that she was deeply concerned.

I sighed deeply. "I have the restraining order."

"I don't know if a restraining order gonna keep that boy away." Mama put her fork down and waited for me to look up at her. "Don't you go nowhere by yourself, Dee-Dee."

"But if I get accepted into the program, I'll have to go to school and I have to work…"

"I mean you need to make sure you always have people 'round you, so if you ever need help you won't be alone."

Was Rodney really that crazy to try to do something to me if he caught me alone? I shivered as I thought about how Walter had to rescue me in Tennessee. *Better safe than sorry*, I thought sadly. He wasn't remorseful at all and believed that he was justified in what he had done to me. There was no way that we could get back together as long as he felt that way. I did not want to end up like his mother.

I had gone to see her a couple days after returning home to return Rodney's suitcase. Mrs. Jackson was clearly upset when she found out that I had left her son. She acted as if I was the one responsible for the problems we were having.

"How can you just leave your husband," she demanded. "The

two of you are one in God's eyes. The wife's duty is to obey her husband Dee-Dee. You need to go back and submit yourself to your husband."

"Mrs. Jackson, Rodney almost killed me."

She stared at me in disbelief before finally saying, "But he didn't kill you, did he? All couples have their problems. We as womenfolk are a lot stronger than we think. God didn't let him go too far. He is still your husband Dee-Dee. I know what he did hurt you. I been there a time or two myself, but you have to remember the vows that you made before God. You need to go back home!"

It was as though she hadn't heard a word that I had said about how her son had treated me. "Your son almost killed me," I repeated.

Mrs. Jackson went on and on about how I couldn't just think of myself anymore and I should be thankful for a husband who did his best to provide for me so that I could stay home and be the keeper of the house the way the Bible say.

"Mrs. Jackson," I interrupted, "I understand that Rodney is your son and you love him, but I can't go back to him if he's going to mistreat me. I just wanted to bring his suitcase to you so that you can give it to him the next time you see him."

She grabbed my arm as I turned to leave. "Chile, I know you young people want life to be easy and ya'll not willing to put up with a lot of things these days, but the best thing you can do is go back to your husband. God put the man in charge of the woman. You need to be there for your husband. You don't want to be the one responsible for him turning to another woman do you?"

My jaws dropped open as I stared at the tall lanky woman glaring down at me.

"He's already been with another woman. He was sleeping around while I was up there trying to be a good wife to him," I said matter-of-factly.

Mrs. Jackson's grip remained firm as she held my eyes. "But he always came back home to you didn't he?"

I pulled myself away and moved to the door. "I'm sorry Mrs. Jackson. I think I deserve better than that. I have to go. Ms. Lucille is waiting for me in the car and I don't want to keep her waiting."

"I will be praying for you and Rodney to work things out and get back together," she said behind me. "It just ain't right for a man and a woman to be separate from each other. You're down here and he's up there. You need to be up there taking care of your husband."

"Goodbye Mrs. Jackson." I waved quickly as I ran down the steps before getting into the car.

Ms. Lucille blew the horn and waved to Mrs. Jackson before backing out of the driveway. "She doesn't seem too happy. What did you say to upset her?"

I shook my head before responding. "She's upset because I left Rodney. She says that I need to go back and take care of my husband because the Bible says the wife has to submit to her husband." I was thrown against the door as the car jerked violently to the right.

"She said what?" Ms. Lucille yelled. "You mean to tell me that old biddy thinks you should keep lettin' her son beat on you?"

I looked wide-eyed at Ms. Lucille as she gripped the steering wheel tightly. "I think that woman got a screw loose. Who in they right mind wanna go runnin' back to a man who beats up on 'em all the time?"

Ms. Lucille fussed about Ms. Jackson all the way back to Mama's house. The conversation was sure to get even livelier once Mama and Ms. Pearl found out what Mrs. Jackson had said. We pulled into Mama's driveway ten minutes later. She was sitting on the porch rocking back and forth in her rocking chair. Ms. Pearl was sitting beside her. Both of them watched us intently when they saw the car pull into the driveway.

I got out quickly and left Ms. Lucille still fussing loudly to herself. As soon as I walked up the steps, Ms. Lucille started talking behind me.

"You never gonna believe what that old bat told Dee-Dee when we went over there."

Mama looked at me with a look of concern. "What happen Dee-Dee?"

I shrugged knowing that there was no point in telling her because Ms. Lucille was going to tell her anyway.

"She had the nerve to try to blame Dee-Dee and told her she need to go back to that boy."

"What! That what she say to you Dee-Dee? Why that woman has lost her mind. Harold been knocking her around so much all her marbles loose in there," Ms. Pearl said before slapping her legs as she laughed hysterically.

"I don't think her elevator go all the way to the top," Ms. Lucille said jokingly.

"Humph, it's a good thing I didn't go over there," Mama said angrily. "I sure would a given her a piece of my mind. Did you tell her what he did to you?"

"I tried to tell her, but she said I should be happy that I had a husband who was taking care of me so that I didn't have to work."

"What," all three of them said in unison. Ms. Pearl slapped her leg again and shook her head.

"So that's the price you pay for a man doing his job?" Ms. Lucille said angrily. "Before Johnny died I never had to work, but I didn't have to put up wid no weekend whippin' parties either."

Ms. Pearl laughed loudly. I could see that Mama was too upset to laugh. She frowned and balled her fists up tightly. "Lawd, I don't know how Dee-Dee got tied up wid such a backward family. I know he better not show his face round here no time soon that's all."

I quietly slipped into the house and left the three of them talking. This discussion was going to continue for awhile. Listening to them only reminded me of how foolish I had been to marry Rodney in the first place. If I had it all to do again, there were so many things that would have been done differently. Unfortunately for me the past could not be rewritten.

Chapter 3

The next day found me sitting next to Mama in Mrs. Jackson's living room. Mama had announced the night before at the dinner table that we were going to pay Doretha Jackson a visit.

"We're what?" I asked incredulously, hoping that she wasn't serious.

"We going over there and talk to that woman about her son. It's time to talk to her woman to woman!"

My jaws dropped. Once Mama made up her mind about something there was nothing that I could do to change it. "But what good could that do?" I asked bewildered.

"I don't know what good it'll do, but I'm doin' it anyway."

Mama picked up her fork and began to stab at a piece of broccoli on her plate. I couldn't think of anything else to say, so I just watched her and thought about what kind of greeting Mrs. Jackson would give us.

And now here we were, sitting in a dimly lit room on the slippery plastic that covered the pale blue loveseat. I remembered this room well. Mrs. Jackson had said that she liked to keep this room clean for company. Apparently, that did not include me. She had politely ushered me out of it the time I tried to read a book in here.

"Did Dee-Dee tell you that you would have a grandbaby by now if it wasn't for your son?"

I held my breath as I waited for Mrs. Jackson's answer. Shock quickly registered across her face and in an instant it was gone. Mrs. Jackson cleared her throat before speaking. "No, I didn't know anything about that. What happened?" She looked at me cynically.

The plastic on the sofa rustled beneath me as I squirmed nervously. *Why did Mama have to bring that up?* It was still hard talking about the baby that I had lost only a few months ago. "I had a miscarriage after Rodney threw me over the sofa," I whispered.

Mrs. Jackson clutched her chest. "Oh my, I'm sorry to hear that. And what made him do a thing like that?"

"Does it matter?" Mama asked tightly. "What gives him the right to put his hands on her?"

Mama was getting angry and she was about to do what she had threatened to do earlier which was to give Mrs. Jackson a piece of her mind. I cleared my throat before continuing. "He was mad because I had bounced a check. He didn't give me a chance to tell him that I had spent the money because I needed some maternity clothes," I added hurriedly.

"I see," Mrs. Jackson said quickly before looking down at the floor.

"I wish you could have seen the way my baby looked when she came back home. He had her face all black and blue. You got three children. I only got this one and I ain't gonna sit by and let your son kill her!" Mama said angrily.

"Well I'm sure it wouldn't have come to that," Mrs. Jackson said quietly, quickly glancing at me before looking down at the floor again. She tugged nervously at the thin gold chain around her neck.

Mama went on as she balled up her fist tightly beside her. "Doretha, I came over here to talk to you woman to woman, one mother to another. I know you love your children and you would do anything for them. What I'm tellin' you is that Dee-Dee is all I got and if that lil narrow tail boy of yours put his hands on her again, I'll put him six feet under." Mama's voice had risen to a feverish pitch by now and there was nothing that I could do to calm her down.

I had begged Ms. Lucille to come in with us, but she had refused. She said she would wait outside in the car. According to her, this was family business.

Mrs. Jackson squirmed and held up her hand toward Mama. "Now calm down Hattie. I understand how upset you must be, but there's no cause to get all worked up."

"The reason I'm upset is because your son think he got a right to do whatever he wants to my baby and get away wid it. He threatening her and telling her he comin' here and takin' her back to Tennessee. What I'm tellin' you is, you gonna have one dead son if he try to put his hands on her again!"

Mama was at the boiling point and Mrs. Jackson could clearly see that.

"I'll talk to Rodney. He can be bull-headed, but I'll have a talk with him next time he calls. It's kinda hard to get in touch with him now that he livin' in the barracks." She glanced at me quickly before looking at Mama. "And besides, I'm sure it will be awhile before he can save up enough money to get another car." Mrs. Jackson looked at me again with a look of accusation before turning her attention back to Mama.

"What happened to his car?" I asked.

Mrs. Jackson seemed surprised that I didn't know. "Well, his commander made him move into the barracks. He say they took a couple months pay and he couldn't make the car note. He had to let it go back when Harold wouldn't send him the money to pay it. We teach our children to handle their own affairs."

No wonder Mrs. Jackson had given me that look earlier. She blamed me for what had happened to Rodney.

"He got what he deserved!" Mama said forcefully. He almost killed my baby and **did** kill my grandbaby!"

It was clear by the expression on her face that Mrs. Jackson did not agree with that last comment. "Now I'm sure that it was an accident, Hattie. Rodney wouldn't have tried to harm his own flesh and blood. He got a rough streak in him, but I'm sure he love Dee-Dee and they can work this thing out."

Mama sighed heavily before answering. "And how is that supposed to happen when he thinks he suppose to beat her when he wants?"

Mrs. Jackson fell silent and stared down at the floor again.

"I want you to know that we got a restrain' order against your son."

Mrs. Jackson seemed shocked. "How they gonna work through their problems if they can't see each other?"

"She gotta do somethin' to protect herself."

"Hattie, I just don't think that's right. Rodney and Dee-Dee are married. All couples have problems, but you can't stop him from seeing his wife."

Mama was extremely agitated. "Doretha, what would you do if it was your daughter?"

I held my breath as I waited for Mrs. Jackson's reply.

"Hattie, I'm not sayin' that it's right for your daughter to be mistreated. I'm just sayin' that the two of them made vows before God. They can't just walk away from that."

"No, you right. They made vows and I don't want to see it end in divorce, but your son can't treat her like a piece of property neither."

The two women went back and forth arguing about Rodney and me. I wondered if they were even aware that I was still in the room.

"Hattie, we gotta stay out of it and let Dee-Dee and Rodney work this out. Do you still love your husband, Dee-Dee?"

I squirmed nervously as both of them looked at me. "Ah, I do love Rodney, but I don't want to be his punching bag either," I said.

Mrs. Jackson looked away briefly before looking back at Mama. "We can't undo what God joined together Hattie."

Mama leaned over to Mrs. Jackson before responding. "You always want to go back to the Bible, well don't the Bible say a man suppose to love his wife? How can you say you love somebody if you keep tryin' to hurt 'em?"

Mrs. Jackson's eyes faltered briefly. "I'm not the expert Hattie. I'm just sayin' we gotta let these two young people work through their problems. It's wrong for a woman to just pick up and leave every time things don't go her way."

Mama shook her head and motioned to me that she was ready to go. I helped her up from the sofa while trying to pull the plastic from the back of my thighs. Mrs. Jackson stood up quickly and walked behind us as we walked to the door.

"Dee-Dee, don't be a stranger now. You can always stop by if you need to talk to me."

"Humph," I heard Mama say under her breath. I nodded my head to let her know that I heard her.

"I'm sure I'll get a chance to talk to Rodney soon and let him know ya'll was here."

"Goodbye Mrs. Jackson." I turned to her briefly before helping Mama down the steps.

"Y'all take care and thanks for stopping by," Mrs. Jackson said as she watched us get into the car.

Mama didn't say anything else until we had pulled out of the driveway. "Talkin' to that woman is like talkin' to a rock!" Mama fumed. "I got no patience for that kinda nonsense."

Ms. Lucille sucked her teeth loudly and shook her head. I told you Harold done knocked all her sense out."

She got the nerve to tell Dee-Dee to stop by if she needs to talk. What she gonna talk about, how to take a lickin' and keep on tickin'? The one she needs to be talkin' to is that scrawny butt son of hers!"

I looked out of the window and listened quietly to their conversation as we headed back home. When we got home, I helped Mama out of the car and onto the porch before going to check the mail. The letter in the middle of the pile caught my attention immediately. I held it in my hands and took in a deep breath. It took only a few seconds to rip the envelope open and scan the contents of the letter.

I hurried onto the porch to give Mama the good news. "I got in for the fall semester Mama!" It was hard to hide my excitement.

"Congratulations Baby!"

Ms. Lucille clapped and came over to give me a pat on the back. "That's real good Dee-Dee. I'm proud of you. You gonna do real good. I been through college myself."

I frowned. "I didn't know you went to college."

"She been to college alright," Mama said.

"I said I been 'through' there. I didn't say I went," she laughed until tears came to her eyes.

Mama looked at her and shook her head. "Lucille, you need help." She turned to look at me. "So when do classes start Baby?"

"I looked at the letter again and gave her the dates. It's a good thing my new job starts next week. Now I can schedule my classes around the hours I have to work and save up some money to buy my books."

"Sound like you got a good plan, Dee-Dee. Things will work out," Mama replied nodding her head.

"What's all this commotion over here?"

I turned to see Ms. Pearl making her way across the street.

"I was wonderin' what was takin' you so long to make it over here," Ms. Lucille said.

"I had a time gettin' my bones to cooperate this mornin'. Ya'll been to see Doretha yet?"

"Lawd, you done miss everything Pearl." Ms. Lucille said. "We been there and back. It was a waste of time going to see that woman," she said shaking her head.

That was my cue to leave before they started talking about Mrs. Jackson again. The discussion would last a good part of the day. I quickly shared my good news with Ms. Pearl before excusing myself. "I got accepted into college," I said cheerfully.

"Why that's wonderful Baby." Ms. Pearl made it onto the porch and came to give me a big hug. "I knew you would get accepted. They'd be crazy not to let you in."

I laughed at Ms. Pearl as I turned to go into the house. "Mama, do you want me to fix some lemonade or something?"

"That would be fine, Baby."

The three women were left to their gossip. Mrs. Jackson's ears would be ringing real soon. I sat down at the table and read the letter again. I wrote down the things that I needed to take care of before I could register for classes. My dream of going to college to study nursing was going to happen after all.

Rodney had been so adamant about me not working. And he

always made up some excuse for me not to enroll in college. "I'm the man. It's my job to take care of you not the other way around," he always said when the topic came up, which wasn't often. He was furious the last time I mentioned working and told me he didn't want to hear anything else about it. Boy, would he be upset to know that I was going to school.

"You finished wid that lemonade Dee-Dee?"

I quickly jumped up to make the lemonade. A few minutes later I took it out onto the porch. "I'm sorry it took so long."

Ms. Pearl got up to help me. She took the glasses from the tray and handed one to Mama and Ms. Lucille. "This is exactly what I need right now. It look like we gonna have another hot one today."

"Yeah, you might be right about that," Mama said as she poured the lemonade into the glass. "Thank you, Dee-Dee. Why don't you bring a chair out the house and join us."

"I'm going upstairs to take a nap. It was hard getting to sleep last night." *Not only was it hard getting to sleep, it was hard staying asleep lately.*

"Poor, Baby, you been through a lot Dee-Dee. Give yosef time. It'll get better soon," Ms. Pearl said sympathetically.

Her words almost brought tears to my eyes, but I gathered myself quickly and waved to them before going back into the house. It was nice that Mama had such wonderful friends who were always there for her.

Francine was my only close friend right now and she was miles away. *I'm going to give her a call and tell her about my good news.* My heart sank after the phone rang several times. She was probably at work at this time of the day anyway. It would have been nice to talk to her right now though.

I lay across the bed to take a nap. It was hard to keep from thinking about the scene that had occurred between Mama and Mrs. Jackson. I knew that Mama was trying to protect me, but it was time for me to handle my own problems. I couldn't let her fight my battles for me. Was there a future for Rodney and me? I wanted my marriage to work, but not if it meant being treated like a piece of property.

Rodney wanted me to be like his mother and just accept anything he did and pretend that it was OK. I couldn't live that way. We had lost a baby because of his temper. What would he do the next time he got mad? As I continued to think about the problems and the best way to handle them, my eyes grew heavy and it wasn't long before I was fast asleep.

❧ *Chapter 4* ❦

It didn't take long for me to settle in nicely as a college student. I loved being in college, but it wasn't easy trying to work and go to school full time. I had met a lot of girls my age, but I was reluctant to hang out with them. Most of them were only concerned about partying and they often skipped classes because they were hung over from the night before. They seemed surprised when their invitations for me to join them were turned down. I was so tired when I got off from work that going to a party was the last thing on my mind. Besides, that type of lifestyle no longer interested me.

"You workin' too hard Baby," Mama would say when I dragged myself in and plopped down on the sofa beside her. The job at Woolworth's didn't pay much, but it was enough to help me pay for the things I needed for school and to buy a used car from an old lady at church. Being able to live at home with Mama was also saving me a lot of money.

It was still hard to believe sometimes that I had a car of my own. The little white Mazda was pretty beat up, but it was mine just the same. Mama had pitched in to help me buy it because she didn't like the idea of me waiting alone at the bus stop. She had called Mr. Perry, one of the deacons at church to go with me to check the car out before I bought it. She wanted to make sure that I wasn't buying a lemon.

I was so proud of myself when I drove home in my little car. Ms. Pauline didn't want much for it. It had belonged to her husband before he passed away three years ago. She said there was no point in having the car just sitting there in the yard. She was happy that someone else would be able to use it. I could hardly contain my excitement. I took Mama for a ride as soon as I got home. As we drove past Woolworth's, I slowed down and blew the horn at Sharon, a fellow-worker, as she was about to enter the store. I waved wildly when she turned around to see who was trying to get her attention. I stopped the car and blew the horn again.

"Hey Claudette, look at you. You finally got that car. Good for you girl," she yelled, smiling brightly.

"Thanks I'll see you tomorrow."

"She seems nice," Mama said as she struggled to get comfortable in the tiny passenger seat.

"Yeah, Sharon trained me on the cash register when I first started working there. I know things must be hard for her trying to work, go to school and take care of her two year old son."

"Where's the daddy?"

"He gives her money, but he doesn't claim the baby as his," I answered hesitantly. "He's married." I waited for my words to sink in before looking at Mama. She was shaking her head from side to side.

"That must have broke her Mama's heart," Mama said sadly.

"Yeah, it did. Sharon said her Mama was real mad when she first found out and wanted to take him to court for child support, but she begged her not to."

"Well I can understand that. It's his responsibility too to help take care of that chile." Mama squirmed in the seat again as she fidgeted with the seat belt.

"His wife doesn't know about the baby and Sharon didn't want everybody in the neighborhood to know about the affair."

"Seem like she waited too late to think 'bout that. Now that chile' gonna be raised wid out a daddy." Mama shook her head again. "Lawd, if people would only think first before they get into these things. But we all make mistakes. I pray she get on her feet and make a good life for that boy."

We were both silent as I drove around Hampton Park. "You want to get out for a bit and walk around the park?" I asked.

Mama squirmed again. "No. I think I had enough sightseeing for one day. I'm ready to get out of this little seat," she said smiling.

We laughed as we headed home.

"How Cynthia comin' along? I ain't seen her come by the house in a long while." Mama glanced over at me quickly.

I breathed in deeply. "Cynthia still likes to party a lot and I really don't want to go to the clubs anymore. And when would I have time to go out anyway? The only thing I can think about now is work and school."

Mama nodded and smiled. "She doing alright?"

"Yes. The last time we talked, she said she was looking for a shop, so she could get out of her mother's basement."

"That must mean she makin' pretty good money doing hair then?"

"Yes. She says the pay is real good."

"That's good. Her momma was real disappointed when she dropped out of college. That was all she talked about at church, how her baby was the first one in the family to go to college." Mama was silent for a few minutes before adding. "I sure hope you stay in there 'til you get that degree. Companies these days lookin' for that piece of paper and you can't get no good job wid out it."

We pulled into the driveway. "I have no plans to quit Mama, so you can stop worrying about that."

I got out of the car and went around to the passenger door to help her out. She grunted a few times before she was finally able to pull herself up out of the seat.

"You got a nice car Baby, but I don't think I'll be ridin' around in it too much," she said as she slowly shuffled to the porch.

"I like your car Dee-Dee. That's real nice," I heard Ms. Pearl say as she came up behind us.

I turned to smile at her. "Thanks, Ms. Pearl. I'll have to take you for a ride sometime."

"Yeah, I'd like that." She walked around the little car looking in the windows at the seats. She came up onto the porch.

"Yeah, she got a nice car, but it's a bit too tiny for me," Mama said huffing.

Ms. Pearl laughed and sat down beside Mama. I looked in the mailbox to see if we had anything. A letter from Rodney was at the top of the pile. I stared at the letter for a few seconds before I slipped it into my pocket and flipped through the rest of the mail. I handed the letters to Mama and left the two women on the porch.

The letter stayed in my pocket until I reached my bedroom. It was a bit surprising that Rodney would write me. I was sure that it was because it was the only way he could have any contact with me since I was refusing to talk to him. He had threatened me several times and not having to talk to him gave me time to try and figure out what to do about our situation. Maybe he was getting the message that I wasn't playing around when I said things had to change in our marriage.

Looking at his letter gave me mixed feelings. *Was he finally trying to make amends?* My heart raced wildly as I quickly opened the envelope. I read the letter slowly hoping to find words from a repentant husband begging my forgiveness for all that he had done. Instead, there were the same familiar accusations and words from a man who was refusing to accept responsibility for his actions. He said that I was acting like a baby by running back home to my mama and not trying to work our problems out. He accused me of wanting to end the marriage so that I could party all night with my friends and be with other men. There were no words of endearment or anything to indicate that he even missed me. He seemed more concerned about getting me back in line so he wouldn't look weak.

I was furious. I was glad that I hadn't shown it to Mama. She would get all worked up about it. I balled the letter up and threw it on the floor and sat there shaking my head angrily. It was obvious that Rodney had no intention of changing and he was only interested in his ego. I fumed and took my frustrations out on my pillow. We hadn't seen each other for almost four months and the last time we talked was nearly three weeks ago. I was rarely at home to answer the phone and Mama didn't bother to tell me when he called. She did tell me when Francine called, but I hadn't found the time to call her either.

I smiled when I remembered how happy Francine had been when I called her after I got my letter of acceptance into college.

"I knew you could do it Claudette! That is great news."

We had talked for nearly half an hour before I thought about the phone bill and told her we had to get off the phone. We both laughed when we realized how long we had been talking. I always paid Mama for the calls as soon as the bill came, but I didn't want to run it up too high.

I picked up the phone and dialed Francine's number. I was supposed to be studying for my math test, but I really wanted to talk to her and tell her about my car. *Please be home.* The phone rang three times before she picked it up sounding out of breath.

"Hello?"

"Hey, it's me."

"Claudette, it's good to hear from you. How are you?"

I settled back against the headboard and brought her up to date on all that had been happening. She sucked in her breath when I told her about Rodney's letter. "Girl I don't know what that boy is thinking. Seems like he would be doing everything he could to get you back. Have you thought about what you want to do?"

"No."

"The only thing you can do is pray and ask God to help you through this. I know it's hard. Did you try to talk to your pastor about it? You could try going in for some counseling and see what he says."

"No, I've been working a lot of weekends lately," I said hurriedly. Trinity was my home church; I didn't look forward to going even though it was the church I had attended for most of my life. The services seemed so dry and dull and the majority of the congregation was close to Mama's age or older. Most of the young people had moved away and only came back to visit during Homecoming. It was nothing like Francine's church. I hated to admit it, but there were times when I was happy when I worked on Sundays, just so I wouldn't have to go.

"When you get some time you really should go by and talk to the pastor. I'm sure he would be able to offer some advice."

I thought about Francine's words.

"I'm just happy that you are out of harm's way. At least this little separation gives you some time to think it all through. Oh, girl, I forgot to tell you. I called you last weekend to tell you that I saw our little friend at the pizza shop on post last Friday."

Who was she talking about? She couldn't be talking about Walter because she saw him every Sunday at church. "Who are you talking about?"

"I saw Teresa Collins with some other guy. I wasn't sure it was her at first because it was hard to get a look at her that night at the bus station, but the guy that she was with called out to her to find out what kind of drink she wanted. They were sitting at the table across from me and I saw the last name on her nametag. The two of them looked all lovey-dovey. She was practically sitting in his lap."

I was stunned to hear that Teresa had moved on so soon. "Things must not have been that serious for her and Rodney. She wasted no time in moving on after she managed to help to ruin my marriage," I said angrily.

"You should have seen her," Francine said quickly. "I wanted to tell her what I thought of her, but I held my peace."

"Hopefully, she hasn't moved on to somebody else's husband," I said sarcastically.

"Let's hope not," Francine said. "She's a hussy if I ever saw one."

I laughed. "A hussy, where in the world did you come up with that?"

Francine laughed too. "I could call her something else, but that wouldn't be nice."

I laughed again. "I'm just glad you were the one who saw her and not me. I'd like to dig her eyes out."

"Yeah, I'm glad it wasn't you either. I can only imagine what that would have been like. She probably forgot all about Rodney and don't even realize the pain she caused."

"She didn't make him cheat. He obviously wanted to do it." My heart still ached when I thought about the day that I saw her kiss Rodney in the parking lot.

"She needs to know that it's going to come back to her though. One day she's going to have a husband and feel the pain she caused you. What goes around comes around. You can believe that," Francine said firmly.

We chatted for the next fifteen minutes. I was reluctant to ask her about Walter, hoping that she would somehow get around to mentioning him. I often wondered about how he was doing and prayed that he had forgiven me. My behavior was shameful. He was a good man. It was hard to hide my disappointment when I hung up the phone.

I sat there for a few minutes thinking about our conversation. It was good to know that Rodney was no longer with Teresa, but I couldn't help but wonder why he brought her to the bus station that night if he wasn't that serious about her. I fell back onto the pillows and stared up at the ceiling and thought about Rodney. I really needed to study for my exams, but I couldn't keep my eyes open. Working and all the late night studying had caught up with me. I could feel myself drifting off to sleep.

❧ Chapter 5 ❧

The heat outside was stifling. The street that was normally filled with kids playing tag, double-dutch, hide-and-seek, and the other childhood games that I used to love so much, was deserted. There wasn't much to do on a day as hot as this. My hair was clinging to the side of my face. I was thankful when the temperature inside of the car finally began to cool off. The sweat on the nape of my neck where the hair hung loosely started rolling down my back.

I drove around town for a few minutes and found myself driving near Trinity. The small church had been built over eighty years ago and was in need of a lot of renovation. But the stained glass windows were beautiful and my eyes were often drawn to them when I found my mind drifting during one of Pastor's really long sermons. There were only three cars in the parking lot. It was time to take Francine's advice and go in and talk to Pastor West.

As I sat in the parking lot looking at the building, I thought about the times when I had to stand in front of the church to recite a memory verse and tell the congregation what I had learned in children's church. Speaking in front of people was challenging for me. A brown stain in the red carpet became my focal point as I quickly blurted out the scripture and verse.

Cynthia on the other hand would always gripe and complain. She always tried to convince our Sunday school teacher, Ms. Shelia, to let her go to the bathroom right before we were ushered to the front of the church. Cynthia had a hard time remembering her scriptures and the other children would have to help her finish the verse. Her mother would clap loudly for her whenever she recited the verses without making a mistake. Ms. Shelia would give her the shortest verses, but by the time we made it to the main sanctuary, Cynthia had usually forgotten it. I always tried to stand close to her so that I could tell her the parts that she forgot.

I got out of the car and hesitated before walking into the church.

Suddenly, I was having second thoughts about my decision to come here. Ms. Helen was sitting at her desk when I walked into the little office. She smiled brightly as soon as she looked up and saw me.

"Dee-Dee, how are you doing Baby?" She got up quickly and came around the desk to give me a hug. "Lawd, it's so good to see you. I never get a chance to come over and talk to you on Sunday's. I'm always so busy with the Pastor's Aid Committee. So what brings you here this time of the day?" She looked at me curiously.

I immediately regretted my decision to come without calling to make an appointment first. "I'm sorry for not calling. I just wanted to talk to Pastor about a few things. I can come back later if he's busy." I looked at her face quickly to see if she disapproved of me being here.

Ms. Helen nodded quickly. "Yes, he's in. Let me check with him and see if he has some time to meet with you. Sit down over here and I'll be right back."

I sat down in the chair that she pointed to and began twirling the strap on my purse nervously. *What was I going to say to Pastor West?* My mind raced wildly as I thought of how I would start the discussion. Ms. Helen was back before I could figure it all out. Before she could say anything, I could see Pastor West following closely behind her.

"How you doing Dee-Dee?" It's good to see you. Pastor West grabbed my hand as I got up from the chair. I smiled when I looked into his warm brown eyes.

"I'm fine Pastor. I'm sorry to just show up like this, but I needed to talk to you about a few things."

Pastor nodded and ushered me into his office. "It's good that you came by. I love having the chance to talk to my young people. I rarely get the chance to do that. Come on in and sit down."

He ushered me to a comfortable brown leather chair across from his desk. I cleared my throat and thought about how to begin.

"Well, I just wanted to ask you something that's been bothering me and I'm not sure how to handle it." I looked down at the floor quickly and plowed ahead. "I...Well...I don't really know how to start." I looked down again.

Pastor West leaned in toward me and held up his hands. "Why don't you start by telling me how you've been?"

I knew he was trying to put me at ease and for that I was thankful. "I'm fine, I guess."

"You guess?" He looked at me quizzically. "How's your husband?"

I avoided his eyes and quickly shook my head. "I believe he's fine. We have been having some problems and that's why I need to talk to you." I squirmed in the chair and fiddled with the strap on my purse again.

"All young couples have problems Dee-Dee. Are the problems serious?"

I waited a second before nodding. "I left him and came back home because he was…he was hitting me," I said softly. It was embarrasing having to admit this to him.

Pastor West nodded. "I see," he said as he waited for me to go on.

"He was also cheating on me."

Pastor West rested his chin on his clasped hands. He seemed to be deep in thought as I squirmed nervously waiting for his answer. "Dee-Dee, I'm sorry to hear this. I'm glad you came to discuss this with me. It must have been very hard for you to leave. So have you thought about what you want to do?"

I shook my head. "No sir. That's why I came. I love him, but I don't want to keep going through the same thing."

I searched his eyes for signs that he understood.

"I don't blame you. I wouldn't want to have a daughter of mine go through that either. Are you thinking about divorcing him?"

I nodded. "Rodney doesn't think that what he's doing is wrong," I said strongly searching his eyes to see if he agreed with me.

Pastor West cleared his throat before responding. "Well divorce should be the last resort. God hates divorce. Have you considered counseling?"

I shrugged. "I don't think Rodney would go."

Pastor sighed. "I know it's too late for this, but that's the purpose for getting good counseling before marriage." He sighed again.

Pastor West had been extremely sick during the weeks leading up to the wedding, so Reverend Simmons had performed the ceremony. He had asked me several times before the wedding if I was sure I couldn't wait a couple of months and go through pre-marital counseling first. But Rodney had been so adamant about getting married before he left for boot camp and at the time, I really didn't see the need for counseling.

"I want us to get some help before he comes to get me," I blurted out.

"I am concerned that you are being abused and that your husband is having affairs. Both of these behaviors can be detrimental to your health as well as your peace of mind. When is he supposed to be coming to get you?"

"I don't know. I enrolled in college and I have a job." I looked up at Pastor sheepishly.

"So you don't want to go back with him when he comes?"

I shook my head. "I don't want to go back into the same situation," I whined.

"The fact is that you are married to this man and you need to figure out what your options are. You say you still love him. That's a starting point, but marriage is also about commitment. I'm not encouraging you to continue to put yourself in harm's way." Pastor West held my eyes to see if I understood what he meant. "I don't condone divorce. Marriage is about being in covenant with someone. Covenants are not meant to be broken. The Bible gives an exception for cases of fornication, but some couples are able to work through that as well."

I nodded and listened as Pastor West continued.

"Too many people are too quick to get divorced these days and I don't agree with that. With God all things are possible, but you have to have two people willing to make it work. Sad to say, there are times when you have to separate yourself from someone who is dangerous. Having a husband who is beating up on you is not about love. It's about control. People who need that kind of control are insecure. But from what I hear about that family, the apple didn't fall far from the tree".

Pastor West gave me a penetrating look. "Mama said the same thing," I said. "She tried to talk me out of marrying Rodney, but I didn't listen."

Pastor West sighed. "And that's the problem with most young folk. You think your elders are trying to spoil your fun and keep you from something, when they are trying to protect you. But we won't dwell on that. What's done is done. The problem is how to fix what's broken. For situations like this, we have to go to God for the answer. He is the only one who can change hearts."

I nodded.

Pastor West went on, "Jesus says that infidelity is grounds for a divorce, but only because of the hardness of people's heart. Sometimes it's hard to forgive someone when they hurt you in that way. Your trust in your husband has been compromised. That doesn't mean you have to divorce. I cannot tell you the number of couples who have come to me with similar problems, but because they were both willing to work together to save their marriage, they worked it out."

Pastor West sat back in his chair and rocked gently. "The domestic violence is another concern. A lot of women are dead because they decided to stay in a relationship with an abusive man. I don't want that to happen to you Dee-Dee. I don't condone a man hitting a woman and I'm proud of you for doing something to get yourself out of there. That must have been difficult. How did your husband react when you left?"

I told Pastor West about the days leading up to me leaving and about the last conversation I had with Rodney. His expression told me that he was deeply upset.

"God was most certainly with you to bring you through all that. After hearing that, my advice to you is to not go back until there is a change. The Bible says we have to bring fruits of repentance. That means when someone has done you wrong, there should be outward signs of a heart that has changed."

Pastor West held my eyes. "You no longer have a daddy, who can stand up for you, but you got a church family here and we will rally around you and do what we can to help. I know your daddy would want somebody to step in and protect his little girl." Pastor West was silent for few seconds as he continued rocking in his chair. He brightened suddenly and sat up in his chair. Do you mind me sharing this information with Deacon Harris?"

I shook my head. "No sir. I don't mind."

"I want you checking in with him on a weekly basis. I will be calling to check on you myself. Deacon is a good man and he won't take no mess from this young whipper-snapper. He'll know how to bring him to task if he shows up here with that mess. You already contacted the authorities I hope." Pastor West gave me a hard look. He nodded his head when I told him that I had gotten a restraining order against Rodney.

"Well, I will have Deacon Harris check to see how long those things are in effect. We can't have it expiring just when you need it most. Hopefully, the outcome of all this will be that your husband will be willing to get some help and come in for counseling so we can save this marriage." Pastor West looked at his watch quickly. He stood up. "I have to run. I have a meeting across town in about thirty minutes. I am going to follow up with you Dee-Dee and Deacon Harris will be contacting you shortly. Let me pray with you before you leave."

Pastor West reached for my hand and prayed for me. After the prayer, he walked me to the door. "Don't worry. We will help you as much as we can through this."

"Thank you Pastor West. I appreciate all of your help." I smiled and tried to hold back the tears when I walked out of his office. I was seeing him in a different light. As a child, there was never a need to talk to him about anything of a personal nature. I waved to Ms. Helen as I walked out of the office, happy that I had listened to Francine.

On the ride home, I realized that my reluctance in contacting the pastor before had more to do with my pride than anything else. I'm sure it was what had kept me from talking to Cynthia about it. I didn't want anyone to know how foolish I had been in marrying the man they had warned me about.

༺ *Chapter 6* ༻

Mama looked at me quizzically when I walked in the house. She waited for me to come into the kitchen to sit down before she said anything.

"You seem happy about somethin'."

I nodded. "Yes, I went and talked to Pastor West today. I told him everything, well almost everything. I didn't tell him about the baby. He said I am doing the right thing by not going back to Rodney until he gets some help and we go to counseling. I wish I hadn't skipped the pre-marriage counseling sessions. We were in such a hurry to get married that and I didn't think we needed it. Now I see how valuable it would have been to go through that."

"It would have been good, but don't beat yosef up about that Dee-Dee. Lots of people going to marriage counselin' these days still end up divorcin'. I don't know how much good it would a done you anyway. You were so bent on marryin' that boy, you couldn't see straight."

Mama was right. I wouldn't have listened to the pastor. The signs were there early on about how controlling Rodney was and I had ignored them all, believing that he wouldn't turn out like his daddy. Never did I think he would hurt me if he really loved me. *What a fool!*

"Come on now. Don't look so down. Put that smile back on your face. What else did Pastor say?" Mama smiled and patted my hand.

I told her what we had discussed and how he wanted Deacon Harris to start keeping an eye on me.

"Mama nodded her head enthusiastically. "That's good to have a man to stand up to him. Although a buckshot between his eyes would do a pretty good job too."

We both laughed. We stopped abruptly when we heard the light tapping at the door.

"I'll get it," I said getting up quickly from the chair. I could see Ms. Pearl's tiny gray head waiting at the door. She walked in as soon as I opened the door.

"How ya'll doing," she said as she brushed past me and made her way into the kitchen.

Mama and I answered in unison that we were doing fine.

"It's good to see you up and around. You feelin' better?" Mama asked.

Ms. Pearl nodded. "I'm comin' along. It musta been that fish I ate. One mind say not to eat that fish. It didn't look all that good."

"Well why did you buy it Pearl?" Mama asked.

"I don't know. I guess all the other ones Leroy been bringin' was pretty good. I just figure it would be OK."

Mama shook her head. "Knowin' Leroy, he probably left that fish out and didn't pack it in ice like he should."

"Yeah, well I learned my lesson," Ms. Pearl said as she took a seat at the table.

The conversation about Leroy and the fish continued, so I made my escape. "I need to go and get some studying done before I go to work this afternoon. I'll be in my room." I quickly ran up the steps to my room and prepared to spend the next hour studying. The book was where I thrown it beside my bed. As soon as I got settled, the phone rang. I knew that Mama would get it fearing that it was Rodney.

"Dee-Dee, pick up the phone," she yelled. I sighed and reached for the phone.

"Dee-Dee, this is Doretha Jackson. I was wonderin' if you had some time to stop by for a little bit. I want to talk to you about something." I was more than a little surprised that Rodney's mother would call me and that she even knew our phone number.

"Mrs. Jackson, I have to go to work in a little while." I was hoping she would say never mind or just tell me what she had to say over the phone.

She hesitated before continuing. "I won't keep you long. If you could just stop by on your way to work…"

She was waiting for my reply. *I can't just turn her down*, I thought anxiously. "I guess I could stop by for a few minutes," I said trying to hide my frustration.

"Good, then I'll see you in a little while," she said before hanging up quickly.

I sat there stunned. *Why did she need to see me? Did something happen with Rodney?* For the next few minutes, I sat there staring at the wall. I couldn't concentrate, so I closed the book and threw it on the bed. I decided to get dressed for work and head over to her house. *Maybe she wants to drill me some more about my decision to leave her son.*

Mrs. Jackson was looking through the tiny glass in the door when I pulled up in the driveway. I took a deep breath and got out of the car. She had the door open when I got to the top step.

"Thank you for coming. Come on in."

I stepped in as she stepped back from the door. My entire body froze as I looked into Rodney's steely eyes. I dropped my purse, and remained rooted to the spot where I was standing. He walked toward me with a twisted smile plastered to his face.

"Now how is my beautiful wife doing?" I could only stare at him.

"Now Dee-Dee, I know you are probably a little upset with me, but I **do** want to talk to you," I heard Mrs. Jackson saying behind me.

Rodney pulled me to him and kissed me lightly. "I missed you Dee." He looked down at me and brushed my hair away from my face. "Don't be mad at Mama. I had to see you and I knew your Mama wasn't going to let me near you."

I still had not uttered a single word. I was in shock. *How could Mrs. Jackson do this to me? Was she listening when Mama and I had come to see her?*

"Now sit down you two. I want to talk to both of you." I could feel my legs move forward as Rodney held my hand, but I was mute.

"You alright Baby?" Rodney looked at me questioningly.

I sat down next to him on the sofa and turned to Mrs. Jackson as if in a daze.

Mrs. Jackson looked at me and then at Rodney. "Now I know the two of you been through a lot and I agreed to do this when Rodney asked me too, because I don't believe you two ought to give up on your marriage. I know ya'll can work this out if you really work at it." She looked at me pleadingly. "Dee-Dee, I know my son hurt you." I could feel Rodney stiffen beside me. "You've only been married a year. The Good Book say, 'what God joins together let no man put asunder.' Can't you try it again?" She waited for my answer.

I could feel Rodney watching me too. I didn't know what to say and I felt terribly confused right now. Tears were beginning to cascade down my face. There were no words for what I was feeling right now.

"Don't cry Dee. Come on. We can work things out like Mama said."

I shook my head hoping it would help to clear the fog in my brain. "I don't know what to say Mrs. Jackson." The tears were still trickling down my face.

"I'm sorry to put you on the spot like this. My mama did the same thing to me the time when I left Harold soon after we got married."

"What? You left Daddy?" Rodney's voice registered his surprise.

Mrs. Jackson looked down ashamedly. "I never told you kids about this, but yes, when I was pregnant with your brother, Harold Jr., I left and went home to Mama and Daddy."

I quickly swiped the tears away waiting for her to tell us the rest of the story.

Mrs. Jackson looked at me. "I know what you going through Dee-Dee 'cause I been there. I know it's hard. I wanted my parents to take my side against Harold, but they both told me that I was a married woman and not their little girl anymore. Harold was my husband they said, and I needed to go back home to him and make it work." She looked down briefly at her hands clasped in her lap and then back at us.

Mrs. Jackson looked like she was fighting back tears. "My mother took me to our pastor and asked him to pray for me before I went back to Harold. Pastor Shelton prayed for me after he sat me down and told me what I needed to do in order to be a better wife to my husband. Then he told me that God was pleased when I submitted to my husband."

It was hard to listen to her without getting angry. "Mrs. Jackson what about where it says that the husband is supposed to love his wife like Christ loved the church?" I was surprised that I had remembered what Walter had told me. I felt Rodney squirm beside me again.

"I know the Bible say that, but sometime God punish us and that don't mean he don't love us. It's the same between a husband and wife," she said adamantly.

I could only stare at her.

"Now I'm going to give you two a little time alone so ya'll can talk to each other and make things right. I'm gonna go visit Ms. Nell." She stood up and turned to look at both of us. "I want you two to talk, not fuss and carry on. And Rodney, you don't have to handle everything with your fist son. Sometimes you just need to talk about it." Satisfied that she had said what she needed to say, Ms. Jackson walked to the door. She looked back at us and smiled.

"You will thank me for this one day." She walked out the door.

Rodney wasted no time when the door closed behind her. He stood up and pulled me up with him. "I have really missed you Dee-Dee. You have to believe me." He held me tightly and buried his head in my neck. After a few seconds, he held me away from him. "You look good. Look like you lost a few pounds too, but you look good Baby. Come on." Rodney pulled me toward the stairs. I knew he was headed for his old room, the room where we had stayed after we were married.

I felt powerless to pull away. Rodney closed the door behind us and looked at me for a long time. "Dee, my mama is right. We've only been married a year. We can make it work." He pulled me to him again and I suddenly found my voice.

"Not if we don't get some counseling," I said sharply.

Rodney's head snapped up from my neck. "Counseling...We don't need counseling. Now come on over here and welcome me back."

I knew I had to do something fast or I was going to find myself in a position that I didn't want to be in. "Rodney, I'm supposed to be at work in a little while. I have to go."

Rodney's reaction was quick. "I told you before that I don't like the idea of you working Dee." He held my eyes.

I wouldn't back down. "Well I have to work to help pay for my college expenses."

Rodney's eyes narrowed, and then he smiled. "I can see you tryin' to get me mad right now, but I'm not going to let you. Now we agreed to work on this marriage and right now I'm doing my part." Before I could say anything else, his mouth covered mine to stop all protest. I knew that this was one battle I had lost. There was nothing that I could say right now that would deter Rodney from the goal he had in mind.

Two hours later, I found myself sitting at the Jackson's dinner table as Mrs. Jackson placed our meals in front of us. I still couldn't believe that all of this was happening to me. I had been so happy this morning after talking with Pastor West, but none of that had prepared me for the situation in which I now found myself. *How was I going to get out of here and back to Mama's house,* I wondered.

Rodney's father surprised me by doing most of the talking. He grilled Rodney about his plans for a car and getting back on his feet.

"You saving your money?"

Rodney cleared his throat before answering. "Yes sir. I had to spend some of it on the bus ticket to come home this weekend."

He looked at me before looking at his father. "It's been so long since I seen Dee-Dee."

His father grunted before glaring at me. How you gonna work all this out Son?" I could tell that Rodney was not happy with his father's questions.

"I'll work it out Daddy." He glanced at me quickly before he started eating.

"Humph, these kind of things happen when a woman don't know her place!"

I looked down at my plate too afraid to look up at Rodney's father. I could feel his eyes on me as I pushed the food around on my plate.

"At least you trying to hold it all together," he continued. "Just give yourself some time and don't try to rush it all. You don't want to dig a hole for yourself."

I was thankful that Mr. Jackson remembered the food in front of him and brought the discussion to an end. I was beginning to feel sick. I knew I had to get out of here. There was no way I was going to spend the night in this house with Rodney and his family.

After dinner, I helped Mrs. Jackson clear away the dishes. Rodney and his father went out onto the back porch. My mind raced frantically as I thought of how to put an end to this charade.

I dried my hands quickly on the dish towel while Mrs. Jackson put the leftovers away. "I'm sorry that I have to run off Mrs. Jackson, but I need to get home before Mama begins to worry about me."

Mrs. Jackson was busy trying to make room for a pot in the refrigerator. She turned to me quickly and seemed surprised that I was leaving. "Well aren't you gonna stay the night with your husband? He just got here."

The words rushed out of my mouth as I moved quickly to the door. "No. We still need to work on some things." I knew that Mrs. Jackson was trying desperately to get the pot into the refrigerator in order to talk me out of leaving, but she was too late. I grabbed my purse from the sofa and raced toward the door as I heard the lid fall from the pot. I quickly got into my car and backed out of the driveway. I didn't look back.

Chapter 7

My heart was still racing madly when I pulled into the driveway at Mama's house. It would be hard to keep this from her. She was worrying enough about me and this could send her over the edge. *What if Rodney tried to come over here?* The thought sent shivers down my spine. I glanced down at my watch. It was only seven-thirty. I usually didn't get home for another two hours. *What if my supervisor had called to find out why I hadn't shown up for work?* My heart stopped. Mama would be worried out of her mind if Ken had already called the house. What was I going to say? She was sure to question me about coming home so early.

Mama was fast asleep in her rocking chair in front of the T. V. I closed the door quietly to keep from waking her. There was a loud squeak as soon as I reached the third step to go upstairs. I stopped and willed myself not to move.

"Dee-Dee is that you?"

Rats! I came back down the steps. "Hey Mama, I was trying not to wake you," I answered lightly.

Mama reached for her glasses. "I musta dozed off. She looked up at the clock and frowned. "It ain't eight o'clock yet. Why you home so early?" She turned to look at me.

"Just one of those nights," I lied. I immediately felt ashamed for lying to Mama, but right now I didn't want to upset her.

Mama reached for a scrap of paper on the coffee table and squinted as she tried to read it. "Somebody name Sarah called around five o'clock to see if you was scheduled to work today."

It felt as though my heart was going to pop out of my chest.

"I told her that you was on the way. She didn't call back so I figure you musta made it there."

"I had to run a quick errand first." I was digging myself in deeper and deeper.

"Well don't make a habit of being late for work. You don't want to get fired from your job. You want me to heat you something up?"

Mama was about to get up.

"No Mama. I'm fine. I'm not hungry."

Mama turned to look at me again. "You sure nothin's wrong Dee-Dee? You don't seem OK to me. You not comin' down with somethin' are you? I hope you didn't catch what Pearl had." I could hear the concern in her voice.

I laughed. "I'm not sick Mama. You go on back to sleep."

"I'm awake now. I was hopin' to catch Barnaby Jones on one of these channels." She picked up the remote and started flipping through the channels.

I turned to go back upstairs. "Mama, if the phone rings, I'll get it. I'm sure Deacon Harris will be calling soon and I hate for you to keep getting up to answer the phone."

Mama nodded.

"Goodnight Mama. I still got a lot of studying to do."

"Goodnight Baby."

Having to lie to Mama made me feel terrible, but it was the best that I could do to keep her from fretting about me. I raced to my room and immediately picked up the phone to call my job. I waited nervously for someone to answer.

"Woolworth's Department Store, this is Sarah."

"Sarah, hey this is Claudette."

"Claudette, what happened to you? Where are you?"

"I'm sorry I didn't call sooner, but I had a family emergency that I had to take care of. Was Ken mad?"

I held my breath as I waited for her answer.

"Ken wasn't here today. Melanie was in charge and she asked me to call to see why you hadn't shown up."

It was a good thing that Melanie was covering for Ken. He would have written me up for sure. "Would you let her know why I wasn't there? I'm sorry I couldn't get to a phone to call earlier."

"Not a problem. I'll take care of it. You know Melanie's cool. She'll handle it. Gotta go, talk to you later girl."

I hung up the phone and plopped down on the bed. *What a day!* Rodney was sure to be angry with me for leaving, but I just couldn't stay there and pretend like everything was just fine between us. His mother had no right to set me up like that. It was obvious that she would do anything in her power to help her son get what he wanted without regard to how I felt about it.

The phone rang beside me. I dreaded answering it.

"Hello."

"So you waited until my back was turned to make your escape huh?"

He was furious. It was a good thing we weren't in the same room.

"Why would I need to escape? You weren't trying to hold me against my will were you?" I said flippantly.

"Why are you doing this Dee?"

"What am I doing? You are the one who refuses to accept the fact that we have some serious problems that we need to work on." I tried to keep my voice low to keep Mama from hearing me.

"What serious problems? If there are problems, you're not doing much to try to work it out. Why is that? You got somebody else?"

"No Rodney! I don't have anybody else. I just can't go back into the same situation. You think you can hit me whenever you want and you don't see anything wrong with that."

"You act like all we do is fight. The few times I hit you was because you made me do it," he said sharply.

"It's not OK for you to hit me at all Rodney!" I was surprised at the strength of my voice.

"Well stop doing stupid things to **make** me hit you then," he snapped.

"What stupid things Rodney?"

"You know I don't want you to work, but you keep nagging me about it. And every time I go to the field you go out spendin' money and overchargin' our account. You don't think that's something to get mad about?"

I was furious. "I didn't overcharge the account on purpose. You never gave me a chance to explain what happened." I could feel the tears threatening to fall.

Rodney sighed. "I know that now, but I didn't know that then."

"What about your affair with Teresa? What do you have to say about that?" It was a waste of time to try to keep the tears from falling, so I didn't bother to try.

"Here we go again."

"Yes, here we go again Rodney!"

"She didn't mean anything to me. That girl was after me since day one. I don't know what happened. I mean... After you lost the baby, I guess I just kinda lost it."

"And that's why you lied and tried to make it seem like I didn't see you kissing her that day."

Rodney sighed loudly. "Dee-Dee, I already told you, I'm not interested in her. She threw herself at me. What do you expect? I'm a man."

My heart felt as if it was breaking all over again. "I expected you to remember that you are a **married** man."

"I don't want her."

"And that's why you brought her to the bus station that night too, right?

"Let's not bring that up again. I was angry with you for letting Preacher Boy and Francine turn you against me."

"They didn't turn me against you. You did that on your own."

"We are not going anywhere with this. We both did some crazy things, but you gotta believe me Dee-Dee, we can work this out."

I swiped at the tears and closed my eyes. *"God help me figure out what to do."*

"At least give it one more chance, Dee-Dee."

"If you really want it to work then let's go to marriage counseling," I said forcefully.

"We can work it out ourselves," he snapped.

"I talked to my pastor today and he is willing to sit down…"

"Why do you keep tellin' everybody our business? It's nobody's business what goes on in our house."

Rodney was near the breaking point and there was no point in continuing this discussion. "I don't want to talk about this anymore Rodney. You say you want to try, but you don't. You just want things to go back to the way it was and I don't want that. I am not going to be like your mother!" I immediately regretted my words.

"Like my mother…what do you mean **like** my mother? If you were half the woman my mother was, we wouldn't be going through all this right now. My mama don't whine and run away with her tail tucked between her legs over the least little thing," he replied angrily.

Rodney's words stung, but I was determined to stand my ground. "I mean I want to be happy. I don't want to be treated like a doormat." My words surprised me, so I continued. "The entire time that I stayed with your parents, I can't remember your father ever saying anything kind to her. He just expects her to wait on him and jump when he says jump." I knew that I had gone too far talking about his parents that way, but it was too late to take back my words.

"So you want my old man to be some old mamby pamby like your dad was, letting a woman tell him what to do all the time?

My daddy is a man's man. He wears the pants in this house!" Rodney's voice was trembling with anger.

"My father was a good man and he loved my mother. He never raised his hand to her and they had a great marriage!"

There was silence on the other end of the phone for a few seconds. "Look, I didn't call you to talk about your parents or mine," Rodney said tightly. "I want us to get back together."

The softening of his tone caught me by surprise and left me speechless.

"Can we just sit down and talk? I know we can work this out Dee."

"I didn't mean to say anything mean about your parents, but I just don't want to end up like that," I said sympathetically.

"There is nothing wrong with my parents. See, that's exactly what I'm talking about. You do and say things to get me mad and then you make it seem like it's all my fault. Look, I'll be leaving on Sunday and I want to spend some time with you," he said gruffly.

"I have to work tomorrow. I already missed today and I can't lose my job right now." There was absolute silence on the other end. I wondered if Rodney was still there.

"Look, I'm not getting into that with you. Can you come over here? Daddy's going to be using his car tomorrow."

I shook my head in amazement. It was like talking to a brick wall. "Rodney, I just told you that I have to work tomorrow!"

"Well what time do you get off?" He said through clenched teeth.

"Not until five and after that I need to study for my exams on Monday." This was not going over well at all.

"So what you're saying is that you don't want to spend any time with me? Is that it? I came home this weekend to see you!" I pictured Rodney with his hands clenched at his sides.

"Rodney, I can't just pretend that everything is fine, if it's not."

"So what are you saying? You want to end our marriage?"

When I didn't answer he went on.

"I'm not letting you go Dee-Dee. You are my wife and don't you forget it."

"You should know that when I came home in June, I got a restraining order against you." I closed my eyes as I waited for the explosion on the other end.

Rodney started laughing.

"So some piece of paper is supposed to keep me from seeing my own wife," he said incredulously. "Woman please!"

"We need to work things out first before…"

"How are we going to work things out if I can't even see you?"

"I want us to go through counseling Rodney." I heard a loud crash and knew that he had punched something or thrown it to the floor.

"Or what, Dee-Dee, You want a divorce? That's what you want anyway isn't it? Let me make myself clear, if I can't have you, nobody else will!"

His words were chilling. I hung up the phone and took it off the hook to keep him from calling back. Hopefully, no one else would try to call us again tonight. There was no way I'd be able to study again tonight. *What if he showed up at my job tomorrow?* Suddenly my dream came rushing back to me causing me to shiver.

This afternoon at his parent's house was bittersweet. If only things had been different between us. It was hard to admit, but I had missed him. He looked so handsome. I still longed to be with the man that I had fallen in love with and yet, so afraid to be alone with him. I grabbed my pillow and screamed. It felt good to release some of the pent up emotions. This was all so confusing.

We did have some fun times together in the past, but it was overshadowed by his violent temper. This afternoon was different. He had been so tender when he held me. It was that side of him that I loved. But he wasn't always like that. *Why couldn't things be different between us?*

❧ *Chapter 8* ❧

M y head was throbbing the next morning. I had slept very
little last night. *Lord, please help me get through the day.*
Mama would be stirring soon, so I quickly got out of bed, slipped
into my robe and got my clothes ready for work. I especially liked
working on Saturday's because there was no need to worry about
rushing off to work after classes. Satisfied with the clothes I had
selected, I headed downstairs to eat a bowl of cereal before getting
dressed.

Mama found my head buried in the book that I had neglected
all weekend when she hobbled into the kitchen. The pressure was
on and I knew that I would have to cram today and tomorrow if I
planned to do well on Monday. It was obvious that she was aching
pretty badly.

"Good Morning Mama. You need me to get anything for you?"
I felt so bad for her.

"No Baby. I need to take my medicine and get these old bones
oiled up first. But thanks for askin'." She looked up at me with a
concerned expression. "You sleep well last night?"

I was surprised by her question. "Why are you asking?"

"Your eyes look pretty red to me. You sure you not comin'
down wid somethin' Dee-Dee?"

I laughed and shook my head. "I'm not coming down with
anything, Mama. Stop worrying," I said playfully.

Mama rubbed her knees gently and moaned. "These old bones
causin' me some pain today. Look up there and get me my pills and
some orange juice Baby."

I got the pills and handed them to her after taking the caps off to
keep her from having to struggle with them.

"Thank you," she said before sipping the juice in front of her.

"Do you need anything else before I leave?"

"No, you go on. I don't want you to be late for work."

I bent down and gave her a quick kiss on the cheek.

"I'll call you around lunchtime to check on you." *The phone!* I quickly ran upstairs and put it back on the hook before getting ready for work.

"Bye Mama." I said before rushing out the door. I looked around cautiously before going down the steps. Satisfied that Rodney wasn't lurking in the bushes, I hurried to my car and got in. I was taking no chances. Rodney was very upset with me and I had to protect myself. When I made it to work, I followed the same procedures before walking into the building hastily and looking behind me every few seconds.

"Hey Claudette, where were you yesterday? I thought you were on the schedule," Jackie said as she walked toward me.

"I was supposed to come in, but I had a family emergency. I'll talk to you later."

"Hey Claudette, you had a call a few minutes ago. Ken took a message. It's by the register," Sarah said as soon as I walked into the office. I hurried over to the register wondering who would be calling me.

"Thanks Sarah." I found the pink note tucked under the corner of the register. I read the note quickly and frowned. *Why would Mama be calling me already?* I went to the office to return the call.

"Hello," Mama sounded like she was out of breath.

"Mama, it's me. What's wrong?" I was beginning to panic. "That boy showed up here right after you left this mornin'. Did you know he was here?"

I could tell that Mama was extremely upset. "Yes, I knew. I didn't want you to worry, so I didn't tell you. I'm sorry Mama."

"Lawd Chile, why didn't you tell me? I couldn't believe it when he just showed up on my step. I called Deacon Harris and asked him to stop by your job."

Mama was taking no chances on Rodney coming near me. What would she say when she found out I was with him yesterday afternoon? I could see Ken walking toward me and knew he wanted me to open my register. "Mama, I'll call you when I go on break. I gotta go, bye. I'll be alright."

I hung up just as Ken came up. "Claudette, I really need you on your register. Sarah needs some help out there."

"I know. I'm sorry. I'm going over there now." I rushed over to my register and tried to put Rodney out of my mind. I managed to do just fine until I saw him walk in the store ten minutes later. My heart drop to my feet and my hands began shaking violently.

"You got that Claudette?"

"What?" I glanced at Sarah as I tried to tear my eyes away from Rodney.

"We had a price change on item 64. You need to make the change on your sheet."

"Oh, OK. Thanks." I quickly looked at the paper Sarah held out to me and scribbled it down on my sheet.

Rodney walked over to the Deli counter and calmly took a seat. I tried my best to ignore him, but I could feel his eyes on me. *Oh, God help* me, I prayed silently.

I was a nervous wreck, but I managed to get through the first half of my shift with Rodney glaring at me the entire time. It was obvious that he was doing this on purpose to harass me. Now that he knew about the restraining order, he didn't want to risk going to jail, but it didn't say he couldn't sit there and give me menacing looks all day.

I could feel him staring at my back as I hurried into the tiny break room as soon as my shift ended. The tears came as soon I closed the door to the bathroom stall. It took a few minutes to get myself together after that.

When I looked in the mirror, I was horrified. My eyes were puffy and red. I quickly washed my face with cold water and used paper towels to pat it dry. While I was drying my face, Sharon came into the bathroom.

"Hey, what's taking you so long in here? Your break will be over in..." She stopped when she looked at my eyes. "What's wrong Claudette?"

It was hard to keep from crying again when I heard the concern in her voice. "I'm not feeling well."

"I'm sorry. Why don't you see if Ken will let you off early? You want me to go tell him you're sick?"

"No, I really don't want to miss another day of work. I just need to get myself together before I go back out there."

She turned to leave. "Let me know if you need something."

I had to leave the bathroom soon. I tried fanning my face hoping to erase the signs that I had been crying. A few minutes later, I walked out of the bathroom with only ten minutes left for my break. A Coke and a pack of nabs was the only snack I would have time to eat.

"Claudette, there's a man here who says he needs to talk to you for a few minutes, Sharon said pointing to a man by the counter.

I looked in the direction where she was pointing and saw Deacon Harris standing there with his arms folded across his chest.

I quickly got up and walked over to him smiling. "Hello Deacon Harris."

He gave me a quick hug. "How you doing Dee-Dee? Your mama got me up early this mornin'. I tried to call you last night, but the line was busy."

I immediately felt guilty for leaving the phone off the hook. I could see Rodney watching us out of the corner of my eye, but I refused to look in his direction.

"So tell me what's going on. Your mama sounded very concerned when she called me."

"I hate for Mama to worry. She'll be all worked up for the rest of the day."

"Well she's already worked up and wanted me to come and check on you in case he showed up here at your job."

"He's been sitting over at the Deli counter since this morning."

"Describe what he got on," Deacon Harris said without letting his eyes leave my face.

I described Rodney to him and told him what he was wearing. He nodded and rocked back and forth on his heels.

"You go on back to work. I got this."

I immediately felt relieved as I walked back to my register. After a few minutes, I was beginning to feel like my old self again, laughing and making light conversation with the customers. Sharon looked at me several times and smiled. She seemed pleased that I was feeling better.

Deacon Harris walked over to the Deli and sat down next to Rodney. When I looked over a few minutes later, they seemed to be having an intense discussion. It was a blessing that Deacon Harris was here.

"Dee-Dee, I'd like a word with you when you get finished." I turned around to see Mr. Harris leaning over the counter behind me. I finished checking out the last person in my line and walked over to talk to him.

"Is something wrong," I asked before glancing at Rodney briefly.

"I been talkin' to your husband and he seems real disappointed that he come all this way and won't have a chance to spend much time with you. I tried to explain why you didn't want to be alone with him, but he still having a hard time with that. We'll be leaving' in a few minutes. I'm gonna take him back home, but he wants to know if he could talk to you a few minutes before he leaves since he'll be leaving' in the mornin'. Is that all right with you?"

I glanced over at Rodney again. He was staring at me with a blank expression on his face. I looked into Mr. Harris' eyes.

"I know you scared to be alone with him. I won't be far away."

I looked at Rodney again and nodded. "I'm almost finished. I'll be on my lunch break in a few minutes."

"OK, I'll go on back and keep talking' to him. I'll see you in a

...gister just as a couple came to the counter ...teadily until my lunch hour. I tried to quell ...nach as I closed out the register and walked ...rris stood up when I got closer.

...t smoothing' else to drink. I'll be right over He looked down at Rodney before moving f the Deli counter.

...dney and immediately reached for a napkin. ...y hands to keep them busy.

...his Dee-Dee?"

"..."

...'what do I mean'?" he said angrily. "I can't ...y own wife. I gotta get permission before I ...ow are we supposed to work things out if I

...s and saw a mix of anger and pain. "Because ...u hurt me anymore Rodney."

...m like all I do is beat up on you or something. ...nes together. You got everybody thinking' ...er or something. Why do you keep getting ...d in our marriage?"

...ny head. "You don't listen to me Rodney. I keep trying to tell you that we need to get some help."

He curled his fist tightly and I knew he was about to go off again. "OK, what do you think we should do Dee-Dee," he said through clenched teeth.

"Pastor West said he would be happy to counsel us and..."

"And how is that suppose to happen if I'm in another state woman," he snapped. "You expect me to come home every week to talk to some man I don't even know about things that should only be between me and you?"

Rodney was close to the edge, so I thought of what I could say to get him to calm down long enough to for us to talk to each other. "Rodney how can you say you love me when you do things to hurt me? That doesn't sound like love to me."

He seemed lost for words as he looked at me. He shook his head and looked at the soda glass in front of him. "I don't want to hurt you Dee-Dee, but sometimes you just get me so mad and I do things without thinking."

"Well that's why we need to get some counseling. It will help us figure out how to talk to each other without you getting so mad all the time," I pleaded softly.

He sighed heavily. "Dee, we can work things out on our own without all these people getting in our business. We just need to spend some time together."

I could hear the desperation in his voice as he tried to convince me that we didn't need to get help. I felt so sorry for him and wanted to give in and believe that things would be all better if we tried again. He seemed so vulnerable. I wanted to touch him and tell him that everything would be OK, but I didn't.

"Dee, let's just go somewhere tonight and spend some time together. Once we get all these people out of our business things will get better."

He stared into my eyes longingly. I found it hard to breathe. I had to tear my eyes away from his to keep from giving in. Things were so confusing right now. I was struggling with my own emotions. Surprisingly, I heard myself say, "I still think we need to get counseling Rodney. It could help us to have a better marriage."

He ran his fingers through his hair as he stared down at the table. "Don't you remember how good things used to be between us right after we got married? Remember the game we used to play before we'd get out of bed…"

"That's not what we're talking about right now," I said fighting to suppress my emotions. I did miss him and wished that things had turned out differently for us. I took a deep breath when the tears threatened to come.

"Come on Babe. Let's try again. Don't give up on us," he pleaded. He reached over and caressed my hand.

My mind was racing madly. *Maybe things would be better this time.* I could feel myself weakening. I looked into his eyes and knew that I wanted to be with him. As soon as I opened my mouth to say 'yes' the spell was broken.

"Hey Claudette, you got a call. You want me to take a message?" I looked up to see Sharon smiling beside me. It took a few seconds for her words to register in my mind.

"What?"

"You got a call. You want me to take a message?" She looked at Rodney and smiled.

I knew she was waiting for me to introduce them, but I didn't. I got up quickly. "I'll be back," I said to Rodney and hurried to the back of the store. I was out of breath by the time I picked up the receiver. "Hello."

"Hey Baby. I just wanted to call to make sure everything alright." I wanted to kick myself for forgetting to call Mama. The fear in her voice told me how concerned she had been.

"I'm sorry Mama. I meant to call you on my break, but I forgot. Mr. Harris came by. He's still here. Rodney came in a few minutes after I got here. He's been sitting in the Deli all morning. Mr. Harris went over and talked to him." I didn't want to tell her the rest and cause her to worry even more. "I'm fine, Mama."

"Good, I was so worried. You be careful now."

"I will Mama. I'll see you later. Bye."

I hung up the phone and took a deep breath. I looked at my watch. I only had fifteen minutes left on my break and I hadn't eaten anything. I stood there for a few minutes thinking about my conversation with Rodney. I had been so close to giving in. *What am I going to do?* I turned around when I heard the door open. I saw Sharon walking toward me smiling.

"Girl, your husband is **fine**. I bet you hate you had to work today. Why don't you see if Ken will let you take the rest of the day off since he's leaving in the morning?"

I wondered what else Rodney had told her. She knew that I was married, but I had told her he was away on a long field problem. The way she was smiling, it didn't look like she suspected that anything was wrong between us.

"Please tell me he has a brother," she begged as she looked at me hopefully.

"Yes he does, but he's married. Sorry," I said playfully.

"It figures," she said disappointed with my answer. "I guess I understand what the family emergency was yesterday when you didn't show up for work." She looked at me and winked. "I wouldn't have come to work either," she said and began to laugh.

I couldn't help from laughing too. "Girl, you are crazy." I looked at the snack machine and thought about what I could get to curb my hunger until I got off this afternoon. I went over to the machine and dug out the change in my pocket. I got another pack of peanut butter crackers and a Coke. I looked at the clock again and groaned before quickly opening the crackers.

"So you gonna ask Ken about taking off this afternoon?"

I looked at Sharon and shook my head. "No," I said as I quickly covered my mouth to keep the crackers from falling out.

"Why not, your husband is leaving in the morning? If I were you, I would want to spend as much time as possible with a good looking guy like that."

I shook my head and laughed once again trying to keep the crackers from spilling from my mouth.

Sharon looked at her watch. "We got a few minutes left. I'm going to see if they put any more shorts on clearance. My little boy has out-grown most of his clothes. It seems like I'm buying new clothes for him every couple of weeks. I'll see you later."

I waved to her and finished gulping down the rest of the Coke. I threw my trash away and walked back toward the Deli. Rodney's eyes had been glued to the door and his eyes lit up as soon as I walked out. I waved to Mr. Harris as I returned to the seat next to Rodney.

"Who was that on the phone," he asked suspiciously.

"It was Mama. She wanted to make sure everything was OK," I answered.

Rodney scowled. "I guess she thought I was coming here to start some trouble or something right," he asked sarcastically.

I ignored the comment. "Rodney I have to go back to my register in a few minutes. I can understand why you're upset that we can't spend a lot of time together this weekend, but I just want to make sure things are going to change between us. I don't think that can happen without some help." I was relieved that I had sounded so confident.

"Are we going back to that again," he asked irritably. "What do you say about us spending some time together tonight? We been apart so long and we didn't have that much time yesterday at my parents house," he said as he looked at me and smiled mischievously.

I tried not to blush as I remembered yesterday afternoon, but I didn't want to be alone with Rodney right now. He had caught me off guard yesterday. "I really need to study for a major exam on Monday. Maybe I can just call you when I get off and we can talk for awhile."

Rodney's head snapped back as though I had slapped him. "Talk..." He looked at me like I had lost my mind. "I don't want to talk. We've been talking. I want to be with you."

"Well, maybe you can come over later this afternoon," I said lamely knowing he would reject that idea.

"You know your mama hates me. Come on Dee. We need some time alone." He was beginning to lose his patience.

I looked at my watch quickly. "I have to go." I got up to leave and he grabbed my arm.

I could see Mr. Harris getting up from his seat and knew that Rodney saw it too. He let me go and frowned angrily. "Will you talk to me if I call you later," he asked angrily.

I nodded and walked over to Mr. Harris. "I'm sorry you had to spend your time here all morning."

He smiled. "It's no problem Dee-Dee. I agree with your mama. That young man got a lot of anger in him and you need somebody to look out for you. Your daddy and I go way back. I don't know if your mama told you that, but we used to play football together in high school. Now that he's gone, I know he would want somebody to look after his little girl and that's what I aim to do."

I was touched by the sincerity of his words. I smiled. "Thanks Mr. Harris."

He looked over at Rodney and sighed. "I'll take him home now. I can't guarantee that he's gonna stay there though. You need me to come back by here when you get off to make sure you get home alright?"

I didn't want to put him through that. He had already been here all morning. "I can get somebody to walk me to my car," I said, trying to sound confident.

"Are you sure?" He looked at me doubtfully.

I nodded. "I'm sure. Thanks again Mr. Harris." I went back to my register without looking at Rodney. I could feel Sharon's eyes on me.

"Girl you crazy," Sharon whispered to me when I walked

around the counter to my register.

I smiled and walked behind her. I could see Mr. Harris and Rodney walking toward the door. I did not dare look in their direction. I took a deep breath and got back to work.

❧ *Chapter 9* ❧

Mama woke up as soon as she heard me walk in the door later that afternoon. It only took a few seconds to kick off my sandals and plop down on the couch. I lay my head back against the soft pillows and let out a sigh of relief. My stomach growled loudly.

Mama looked at me anxiously. She would want to know everything that happened today with Rodney. "You alright Baby?"

"Yes ma'am. It's been a long day that's all." She listened intently as I told her what had happened at work and how Mrs. Jackson had lured me to her house yesterday afternoon.

Mama had a hard time keeping quiet and it wasn't long before she piped in. "That boy got a lot of nerve. You should a called the cops on him. And I can't believe Doretha did that. She not thinkin' bought your safety at all. She only thinkin' bout her son and makin' sure he get what he want." Mama was furious.

"She told us that her mother did the same thing to her when she tried to leave Mr. Jackson. She said her parents told her that she was married and needed to go on back home and make it work. Can you believe that they would say that to her knowing that he was mistreating her?"

"Unfortunately, that's the way it was back then. People didn't get involved with married folks business and many times men beat those women to death and got away wid it. The law didn't do nothin' bout it neither. The worst part is that they pass that mess on to the next generation."

It was hard to imagine how a man could beat his wife to death. "How could they say they love their wives and do something like that?"

"That's how you know it ain't love Baby."

I told Mama about my conversation with Walter and how he had explained to me that the Bible says that men are supposed to love their wives like Christ loved the church.

She nodded her agreement. "He said right. When a man treats you like you his property, he letting you know he don't really love you. You mean as much to him as the dog and the cat. He might not say it out loud, but that what he thinkin' in his heart. When people do things like that to hurt you, they gonna do it again unless God change their heart."

I thought about her words. "He said he didn't mean to hurt our baby. He said he was just angry that I wasn't there to pick him up from the unit. And then when he got home he found the bounced check."

Mama frowned before replying, "Baby, what's in a person heart will always come out if enough time go by. Rodney's problem is that he grew up seeing his daddy treat his mama that way. That kinda behavior is normal to him."

I nodded, but didn't respond.

"I can't make up your mind 'bout what to do, but if you go back to him wid out him wantin' to change, things won't be different. It won't take long before there will be somethin' else for him to get mad 'bout down the road."

"You're right. It was a good thing that Mr. Harris was there though. He didn't tell me what he talked to Rodney about, but I could tell that Rodney wasn't too happy about it."

"Deacon Harris is a good man. That was nice of him to watch out for you like that."

"Yeah, he told me that Rodney was all upset because he came all the way down here and couldn't spend any time with me. I just wish he was stationed somewhere close so that we could go and get some counseling. It's hard to work on our problems with him being so far away. I just felt so sorry for him today."

"Do you want him to come here?" Mama looked at me anxiously.

I knew she didn't want Rodney here, but she would agree to it if that was what I wanted. "I don't know. He doesn't want to go for counseling and keeps saying we can work through our problems on our own."

"Humph. I bet!" Mama shook her head. "The last thing I want is to come between you and your husband, but I can't stand by and watch him hurt you either," she said adamantly.

"It's so hard to know what to do. I want our marriage to work. I still love him..." I moaned and let my head my fall back heavily on the pillow.

"You in a difficult situation. I can't say I know how you feel cause I never had to go through all that wid your daddy, but I do know what it's like to love somebody wid all your heart."

I looked up at Mama. She had a tight smile on her face. It was clear that she was thinking about Daddy.

"Your daddy was somethin' else. I got weak in the knees every time I saw that man. And when Papa told me I was too young for Earl to come calling", I thought I was gonna die." Mama smiled and shook her head as if she was trying to erase the memory. "We tried to sneak behind Papa's back and see each other anyway, but when he found out, he told Earl to stay away from me and not to come round no more."

Remembering how much Daddy had loved Mama made me smile. He was not ashamed of his love for her and he often let others know that she was the love of his life.

"Earl did everything he could think of to get Papa to change his mind and finally it work. Papa told him to come by one Friday afternoon so they could talk. I was a nervous wreck. Mama told me to stay in my room and let Papa talk to Earl man to man."

This story about my parents was new to me, so I sat up and listened intently.

"That was the longest night of my life, waitin' up there for Papa to get through talkin' to Earl. My sister Helen tried to use a glass to listen through the wall, but she couldn't hear nothin'. They only talk about ten minutes, but it seemed like it lasted forever." Mama smiled. "Your daddy never would tell me what they talk 'bout. He said it was men's business and it had to stay between the two of them."

A few seconds went by before she said anything else. Mama was lost in her thoughts and I didn't want to disturb her.

"Baby, I know your heart tellin' you one thing and your mind tellin' you somethin' else. Nobody can make this decision for you. I just don't want to see you get hurt. I can't stop thinkin' bout the way you look when we come to get you from that bus station." Mama struggled to hold back the tears.

"I'm sorry you had to go through that Mama."

"No, I don't blame you. It was just hard to see you like that and I can't say I ever took a likin' to Rodney. My daddy probably felt the same way about Earl 'til he got to know him and could see that Earl would take good care of me. After that, things were fine between them. But I can't say the same 'bout Rodney. It's hard for a mother to see her baby lookin' like that."

"I know Mama. I want to be with him, but I don't want to go through all of that again either." We were both startled when the phone rang. I had a feeling it was Rodney, so I got up and went into the kitchen to answer it.

"Hello."

"Hey, it's me."

I didn't respond. I looked over at Mama. She got up slowly and walked to the front door.

"I'll be sittin' out here for awhile. I'm sure Pearl or Lucille will be comin' by later."

"Can I see you tonight Dee-Dee? I don't want to go back tomorrow without spending some time with you."

I exhaled loudly. I didn't know what to say. My mind raced furiously.

"Come on Dee. I'm not going to do anything to you. You were here yesterday and nothing happened."

I was torn, but it was hard to trust myself to be alone with Rodney right now. He wanted to continue with our marriage without acknowledging the problems we had and I couldn't live the rest of my life that way. I needed more than he was willing to give right now.

"You still there?"

"Yes, I'm here. It's just not a good idea for us to be together right now Rodney. I don't think that you are taking me seriously about our problems and you want to move on and pretend like everything is just fine. We need help!" His response would not be good, so I waited for the explosive outburst.

It only took a few seconds before I heard glass shatter in the background. Thankfully, I was safe in Mama's house and not on the receiving end of his angry fists.

"I don't know why you keep pushing me Dee-Dee," he said through clenched teeth. "It seems to me like you trying to do things to get me to go off," he said tightly.

"No, I'm not," I said as calmly. "Do you love me?"

"What?"

"You heard me. Do you love me?"

"You know I do. Why are you asking me such a dumb question?"

"You don't show it sometimes. You get angry about the least little thing and always want to control everything I do. How can that be love?"

"Oh, I get it. You got all these marriage experts filling your head with junk and now you falling for it. You are my wife. I married you didn't I? Why would I marry you if I didn't love you?"

"Why would you hurt me if you loved me?"

"Would you get off that? I'm about tired of hearing that. So what, we had an argument or two. I already told you it was an accident about the baby. What else you want me to say?"

His exasperation came across loud and clear. It was obvious that we were getting nowhere with this conversation. "I need to go and study for my test."

"I guess that means you could care less if we see each other after I came all this way to be with you!" he said stiffly.

"No, it just means we are getting nowhere and there is no point in continuing this discussion."

"Dee-Dee, I want to see you."

"That's not a good idea right now," I said before hanging up the phone and taking it off the hook. I went up stairs to study.

Ms. Pearl's short laugh rang out on the steps below. I snatched my books from my backpack and tried to force myself to concentrate on the pages in front of me. It was no easy task trying to get Rodney off my mind, but after a few minutes, I began to focus on my notes.

Forty-five minutes later, I heard Mama calling to me from downstairs. I quickly threw my books to the side of the bed and went downstairs. To my surprise, Rodney was sitting in our living room with a sly smirk on his face.

"Don't be mad, Dee. I just had to see you before I leave tomorrow." He got up and in a few short strides he was standing in front of me. I couldn't believe that he was actually here. Mama probably thought that I had given him permission to come over and let him in the house. Rage began to churn inside of me.

"I said it wasn't a good idea for us to see each other right now," I said forcefully.

"Shh, keep your voice down. You don't want your mama to think we are arguing do you? Come on Dee-Dee. How are we going to work through all these problems you say we have if we can't spend any time together. I won't be able to come back home until Christmas. The least you can do is talk to me for a couple hours. Come on, let's just sit over here." He gently pushed me toward the sofa.

"How did you get over here anyway?"

"My sister Jackie dropped me off. She'll be back in a couple hours to pick me up."

I sat stiffly beside him and glared at the coffee table in front of me. Mama and her friends continued on with their conversation, oblivious to what was going on with us. Rodney reached for my face and turned it toward him. Looking into his eyes right now was the last thing I wanted to do, so I kept trying to turn away. Finally he began squeezing my cheeks and forced me to look at him.

"We are getting back together Dee-Dee, make no mistake about that. I can't get a place for us right now, but as soon as I get all the money saved, I'm coming back to get you. Your place is with me. It's never going to be over, Baby."

There was no mistaking the message that he wanted to convey. The steely eyes locked into mine to make sure that his meaning was clear. I snatched my head back forcefully, to loosen his grip on my face.

I sat motionless as Rodney went on and on about what had happened to him after I left. He whined about the rank he lost, losing his car and having to move into the barracks. He felt that he had already paid the price for what had happened between us and didn't see a need for me to still be upset with him.

Mama came in an hour later after saying goodnight to her friends. Rodney put his arm around my shoulders to give the impression that we were doing just fine.

"Well, I'll tell ya'll goodnight. I'm going upstairs. Ya'll need anything?"

I was suddenly terrified of being left alone with Rodney, but I didn't want Mama in the middle of our mess. I shook my head. Mama turned to go up the steps as a car pulled into the yard. She squinted to see through the tiny slit in the door. "That must be your ride." She glanced at Rodney. The boards creaked loudly as she pulled herself up the steps.

I breathed a sigh of relief when Rodney got up and looked out the window. "She said she would be back in two hours. It hasn't been two hours," he muttered angrily.

I quickly got up and went to the door. Jackie was coming up the steps when I stepped outside.

She smiled brightly. "Dee-Dee, how you doing? Long time no see." She laughed loudly and gave me a big hug.

"I'm fine, how about you?"

"I'm hanging in there. It doesn't take much to make me happy." She laughed a deep hearty laugh.

"I thought you said a couple hours," Rodney snapped from behind me.

"Oh, be quiet brat. You better be glad I brought your butt over here. What I look like, your private cab service?" Jackie looked at me and rolled her eyes. I came back early cause I think something's wrong with that old hooptie. She tossed him the keys. "Take a look and see what's wrong with that thing. There's a flashlight under the front seat."

Rodney huffed loudly as he stomped down the steps.

Jackie looked at me and smiled again. "Sit down and tell me what's been going on with you."

The last time I had seen Rodney's sister was the day before he came home from Boot Camp. Jackie was six years older than Rodney and every time I saw her she had a smile on her face. It wasn't often that I had the chance to talk to her because she didn't visit the Jackson's much. She had said it was because she worked long hours at her job, but I was never convinced of that.

"So my little brother managed to talk you into getting back together after all huh? I'm not surprised. He always manages to get his own way." I glanced in Rodney's direction as he popped open the hood of the car.

She kept going without waiting for my response. "So you going to school and workin' too. Good for you. What you studying?"

I told her about my classes and how much I liked going to school.

Jackie was quiet for a moment before turning to me. "Let me give you a bit of advice Dee-Dee. I didn't say anything at first cause I didn't know if Rodney was gonna turn out like Daddy, but don't you take no mess from him. I watched my mother go through that for years and that's probably why I'm not married today. If a man try to beat on me like that, I'm gonna kill him!"

I could tell that Jackie meant what she said. I nodded to show her that I understood.

"Rodney can be hot-headed. He's been that way since he was little, but you got to stand up to him and let him know you not gonna take that stuff. You hear what I'm saying? He's my little brother and I love him, but if you let somebody treat you bad, they'll keep doing it. You are too young to be going through that. Here let me give you my number if you ever want to talk." Jackie patted her pockets to see if she had any paper to write on. She looked in her purse and found a sales receipt and a pen. She quickly scribbled her number on the paper and gave it back to me.

We both turned when we heard the hood slam. Rodney walked toward us with a scowl on his face. "There's nothing wrong with the car. One of the wires was loose."

"Thank the Lord. I don't need to be paying out big bucks right now to no mechanic. I need every dime I can get," she laughed.

Rodney was not amused. He was clearly upset that we weren't going to have more time to spend together.

Jackie stood up. "Alright, you two say your good-byes so I can get home and get myself something to eat. I'm hungry. I've been out in the street all day." She walked toward the steps and turned to look at me. "Remember what I said Dee-Dee. You got my number. Call me if you need to talk."

She got in the car and started the ignition.

"So what was Jackie talking about?"

I shrugged. "It's just girl stuff."

"What kinda girl stuff?"

"We talked about her job and some other things."

He gave up when he realized I wasn't going to tell him. "I guess this is goodbye for now." He pulled me up toward him and held me for a second. "I'll be glad when we can put all this behind us and get back in our own place."

I listened to him without saying a word. Jackie tapped her horn lightly to hurry him along. Rodney scowled deeply and kissed me. "Well, I better get going before she wakes up the whole neighborhood. He waved and hurried down the steps.

Jackie backed out of the driveway and waved before she drove off. *What a day this had been!* It was good that it was soon coming to an end.

Chapter 10

It surprised me when I walked in from work the next day and didn't see Mama sitting in her rocking chair in the living room or in the kitchen. I began to panic when I remembered that she hadn't answered when I told her I was leaving for work this morning. *What if something was wrong?* I quickly ran upstairs and knocked on her bedroom door.

"I'm home Mama."

"Hey Baby. Come on in."

I breathed a sigh of relief before opening the door slowly. "You alright, Mama?"

"Yeah, I'm fine. I had a hard time last night. I could barely get out of bed this morning. I guess those new pills make me sleepy. I'm gettin' up from here in a few minutes."

"You don't need to get up Mama. I can cook dinner today. What do you want to eat?" I sat down beside her convinced that she had a hard time sleeping last night because she was worried about me.

"No, I had a good nap. I'm feelin' a lot better now. You doin' OK?" She looked at me carefully.

"I'm fine." She nodded and patted my hands.

"Well I'm glad things worked out." There was no point in telling her that I hadn't invited Rodney over last night. She was already stressed out enough. Mama lifted herself up slowly and grimaced. I quickly got up and helped her pull herself up. I knew that I couldn't offer much support, but she finally managed to stand up.

"I'm fine Baby. I'll be downstairs in a little bit. Go on and do what you need to do."

Satisfied that she was OK, I went to my room and thought about everything that had happened over the past few days. It had taken its toll on both of us. I grimaced when I thought about Mr. Harris coming to my job. It was embarrassing to think about how he had to sit there and keep an eye on me. How would I ever be able to face him again? I buried my head in my pillow and groaned loudly.

Mama was obviously feeling a little better. I could hear her singing as she gathered her pots and pans for the meal she was preparing. Thoughts of my wild weekend with Rodney came rushing back to my mind. It was extremely difficult to focus on the notes in front of me as the scene at the dinner table with his parents kept popping up into my head. *I* could feel myself getting angry all over again when *I* thought about the way his mother had tricked me into coming over there. *How could she do that to me?*

I finally gave up and closed my books. Maybe it would be better to take a nap and study later. Mama wasn't the only one who hadn't gotten much sleep last night. The phone rang just as I was drifting off to sleep.

"Hello."

"Hello, this is Mr. Harris. I wanted to check on things. I missed seeing you all at the service today. Is everything alright?"

"How you doing Mr. Harris? Yes, everything is OK. I had to work today and Mama wasn't feeling well."

"Did that young man come by your job today?"

"No, he didn't come back. He was supposed to be leaving out this morning."

"Good. Maybe he listened to me. He was pretty upset when I first tried to talk to him. I finally got him to calm down and he started to listen."

"Thanks for all of your help Mr. Harris."

"No problem. Tell Hattie I hope she'll be feelin' better soon. Don't be afraid to call me if you need me. Take care now."

"Bye, Mr. Harris."

I buried my head in the pillow and screamed after hanging up the phone. It was too bad that Mr. Harris had to be involved in all of this. I closed my eyes and blocked out everything that had happened. I reached for the book again and forced myself to concentrate on my notes.

It wasn't long before my stomach began to growl when the smell of fried chicken filled my room.

"Dee, you 'bout ready to eat?" I heard Mama yell to me from below.

I quickly set the book aside and went to the door. "I'll be down in a minute."

Mama was already sitting at the table when I walked into the kitchen. "Something smells good."

She smiled brightly. "I had a taste for some sweet potato pie today."

My mouth started watering. "Hmm, I can't wait to have some with a scoop of vanilla ice-cream." It didn't take long to fix my plate and sit down at the table. I hadn't eaten since last night and I quickly tried to make up for it.

"Slow down Baby."

I put the fork down and smiled. "Mr. Harris called earlier. He wanted to check on us and he said he hopes you'll be feeling better soon."

"Well that was nice of him to call. He probably got worried when he didn't see me in church this mornin'. What else he say?"

"He just wanted to check on us to see how we were doing." I looked down at my plate and prayed that Mama wouldn't ask any more questions.

"Did you and your husband decide what to do last night?"

I shook my head. Rodney was still living in the barracks, so I couldn't go back to him right now if I wanted to. And there was no way that I was going to drop out of school in the middle of the semester. "We talked, but we didn't make a final decision. Rodney is still living in the barracks and he still needs a car," I said.

Mama nodded. "Just trust God and ask Him to help you to make the right decision." There was apprehension in her voice.

"I will Mama." I picked up my fork again and continued eating. I could feel her watching me, so I kept my head down to avoid looking into her eyes.

Mama sighed and got up from the table. She took her plate to the sink and leaned heavily against the counter. Age was catching up to her. She wasn't getting around as quickly and she had a hard time walking up the steps sometimes. Her curly black hair was now streaked with patches of gray and hung loosely down her back. Daddy used to call her his Cherokee princess. More than a few of the older men at church had an eye for her, but Mama didn't seem to notice. It would surprise me if she ever married again. She was still pining over Earl Chapman, the love of her life. *I hope I'm as beautiful when I get to be her age.*

There was a tiny knock at the door. It was either Ms. Lucille or Ms. Pearl paying her a visit.

"I'll get it Mama." I pushed my chair back and walked to the door. Ms. Lucille was just about to knock again when I pulled the door open.

"Oh, I was wonderin' if ya'll heard me knockin'. How ya'll doin'?" Ms. Lucille was even older than Mama, but she was as skinny as a rail. She was spry for her age and loved to take her afternoon walks around the block. Of course, she spent a lot of time gossiping with the neighbors as she walked her familiar path. There was no doubt that she had some news for Mama and the two of them would spend the rest of the afternoon talking.

It was possible that the topic of discussion would be me. But I didn't mind too much. Ms. Pearl and Ms. Lucille had known me ever since I was born. The two of them loved me as if I was their own flesh and blood.

This was the perfect opportunity to make my escape and get back to my studies. "Mama, I'll do the dishes later. I just want to study another chapter and then I'll come back down for a tiny piece of pie."

Ms. Lucille laughed. "You could probably eat the whole thing and not gain a pound."

I laughed loudly. "Trust me, Mama's tried everything in the book to get me to gain some weight, but I think I'm fine the way I am."

"Dee-Dee is just like Earl. That man could eat like a horse and not gain a pound. All I have to do is look at a pie and gain fifty pounds."

Ms. Lucille and I laughed.

"I'll be upstairs if you need me." I ran upstairs to my room and sat in the middle of the bed before grabbing my book to concentrate on my studies once more.

A few minutes passed by before the phone rang. *Now who could this be? This phone never stops ringing,* I thought angrily.

"Hello."

"Hey, it's me Cynthia. I know it's been a while, but I wanted to see how you were doing."

I had to admit that I was surprised that she was calling, but it was good to hear her voice. "I'm good. I guess it has been a while."

"Yeah, I know. Guess who I saw at the club last night?"

She immediately had my full attention. "Who?"

"Your man was there. Why didn't you come with him?"

My mind raced furiously for an answer that wouldn't make Cynthia suspicious, but I had a feeling she knew something was going on. "I wasn't feeling up to it. I needed to spend some time studying for my exams." There was no way Cynthia would believe me, but I needed to say something.

"Well, Mr. Rodney had them fightin' to get his attention. You know I had to keep an eye on him for you."

I desperately wanted to know if he was with someone, but refused to ask her. "So what were you doing hanging out at the club. You should be tired of playing with those old men by now and ready to settle down."

"Naw, I'm still trying to have me some fun, girl. I'm not getting married until I'm fifty, and besides he has to have at least a million in the bank remember?" She laughed again.

Her laugh was contagious and I found myself laughing along with her. "So, was that all you wanted to tell me?" She probably knew I was fishing for information.

"Um, let me see. I did see your hubby dance a couple times, but it looked innocent enough to me. You know I would have told you if I thought some hanky-panky was going on," Cynthia chuckled.

"Maybe he knew you were watching him."

"That's a possibility. He saw me as soon as he walked in the door. I'm sure he knew he couldn't get away with nothin' around me."

It was hard to keep from smiling. Cynthia always tried to act like she was all hard core, but she was a big scaredy cat. "What's been going on with you? We haven't talked in a long time."

"That's because you went up there to Tennessee and got all spiritual on me. You don't even want to go to the clubs no more. What's wrong with partying every now and then?"

"It's not fun for me anymore, having those dirty old men always trying to come on to you. Half of them smell like a liquor bottle."

"Now you know that's not true Dee-Dee. Some of those guys were fine."

"Yes, a few of them were. I guess things changed for me."

"Well I want my old friend back."

"I'm still your friend. That's not going to change." I had to admit that our friendship wasn't as strong as it was before and I would much rather talk to Francine. There was no way I was going to say that to Cynthia though. She had been a good friend over the years.

"I've been looking for you at church. So why did you stop

coming? You know your mama had you in church every Sunday." I tried to make my voice light and playful.

"Girl, I just don't have time. I'm usually workin' til nine on Saturday's."

"So what you're saying is that by the time you get home and stay out half the night at the club, you can't get out of bed for church on Sunday mornings."

Cynthia laughed. "See you just know me too well. You know how it is. Sometimes I might meet someone and just want to spend some time getting to know him."

"But that's dangerous Cynthia. Some of these guys are crazy. You can't keep sleeping with every man you meet."

"See, that's what I mean. There was a time when I could tell you this stuff and you didn't get all religious on me." It was clear that my rebuke had upset her.

"That has nothing to do with being religious. You are my best friend and I care about you."

"If I was your best friend, I would have known before everyone else in town that you and your husband had split up!"

Her words stung. It took a few seconds before I could think of what to say to her. "Who told you that?"

"Come on Dee-Dee. You know how news travels around here. Everybody knows that you left your husband and you back here livin' with your mama."

"We are just trying to work some things out that's all. And why is everybody in my business?" I replied sharply.

"So it's alright for you to get in my business, but there's a problem if I get in yours?" She no longer tried to hide her anger.

"I'm not in your business. I just don't want to see anything bad happen to you!"

"Look, I'm sorry Dee-Dee. I didn't mean to say all that. I have to admit that I was hurt that I had to hear the news about you and Rodney through the grapevine and not from you."

"You're right. I should have told you instead of trying to cover things up, but I just didn't know how to tell you. I was embarrassed."

"Girl, we've been friends since grade school. Why would you be embarrassed to talk to me?"

"It's just different talking to you about Rodney because I remember how you kept trying to get me to wait and not get married so fast."

"I'm not going to lie to you, Dee-Dee. I did think you should have waited and gone on to college like you planned. After you met Rodney, you weren't the same. You jumped when he said jump and it seemed like he had you wrapped around his little finger."

"You and Mama tried to warn me, but I didn't listen. It was hard to think straight and he kept telling me that we needed to get married before he left for boot camp. You don't know how many times I've wanted to kick myself for not listening."

"I'm not judging you Dee-Dee."

"So who told you that we split up?"

"To tell you the truth, I suspected it when you came back home and couldn't tell me when you were going back and then…"

There was silence on the other end. It was obvious that she didn't want to tell me the rest. "What are you not telling me Cynthia?"

I heard her sigh.

"What?"

"Apparently Rodney has been keeping in touch with Stacy and told her that the two of you weren't together. She told Suzette. You remember Suzette Freeman don't you? Well, she told everybody else."

I felt as though someone had kicked me in the stomach and the air had been sucked out of me. Stacy was the girl Rodney dated in high school before she moved away and Suzette was her best friend.

"Of course I remember Suzette," I said dryly.

"Don't be mad with me Dee-Dee."

I tried to control my anger before responding. "So how long did you know that Rodney was still seeing Stacy?"

"See, that's not what I said. I said he was still keeping in touch with her. According to Suzette, he calls her every now and then."

My mind was racing as I tried to piece together the information I had just been given. "And how long ago was it that Suzette told you this?"

"Come on Dee-Dee. I can see where you going with this. I only found out about that a couple weeks ago when Suzette came in to get her hair done."

"Well, why didn't you call me and tell me!" I shouted. Tears were threatening to spill from my lids, but my intense anger was holding them at bay.

"I was mad at you for not telling me about it when you came home. I just figured you didn't want me to know your business, so I would just keep it to myself."

I didn't trust myself to speak. I closed my eyes as the tears rolled down my cheeks.

"Come on Dee-Dee. That's not fair for you to be mad at me."

Cynthia's words no longer registered. The only thing that was on my mind was the fact that the entire time that we were married, my husband was telling his ex-girlfriend everything that went on between the two of us. *This has to be the ultimate act of betrayal,* I thought.

"Are you still there Dee-Dee?"

There was no use in continuing this discussion with Cynthia. It was impossible for me to think straight right now. "I'll talk to you later. I need to take care of something," I whispered before hanging up.

I fell back on my bed. *I hate him.* I squeezed my eyes together and tried to forget about Rodney Jackson, but it was no use. What a snake. What else didn't I know about him and Stacy? Never in my wildest dream had I even considered that he was still talking to her. Just wait until I talk to him again. He could just forget about us ever getting back together!

❧ *Chapter 11* ❦

The next day was one of the worst days I'd had in a while. The test was a lot harder than I thought it would be. I was sweating bullets when I left the exam room. Most of the answers came quickly, but I had some doubts about my response to the essay question. It didn't help that I hadn't put enough time into studying over the weekend. *There must be something that I could do for extra credit, I thought anxiously.*

Sharon and I pulled into the Woolworth's parking lot at the same time. She waved as soon as I looked in her direction. *She's going to be full of questions about Rodney.* I didn't want to tell her too much about my life, even though she had been very open with me about her relationship with her baby's father.

"Hey, how was your weekend?" She gave me a knowing look before laughing.

"It was fine."

"I bet you hated to see your husband leave?"

I knew she was fishing for information. I smiled and quickly changed the subject. "Did you have an exam today too?"

"I had that dreaded math test today. It will be a miracle if I passed."

Sharon wanted to be a teacher. She felt that a career in education would be best for her as a single mother so that she could have summers free to spend with her son.

"Girl that test was hard. I was one of the last ones out of there. What did you have today?"

We continued to talk about our exams as we walked into the store together and got ourselves checked in. Thankfully, she didn't return to the topic of my husband even though we had plenty of time to chat throughout the day. By noon, I was looking forward to my lunch break. Monday's were typically slow and I just wanted to close my eyes for a bit and try to get a cat nap during the thirty minute break.

At the end of the day, I quickly made my way to my car. I couldn't wait to get home and crawl into bed. I hated having to cram for exams, but Rodney's surprise visit had left me no choice. Mama and her friends were sitting on the porch when I pulled into the driveway. They were laughing loudly when I walked up the steps. Ms. Lucille had probably said something funny. She was a natural comedian, often making Ms. Pearl laugh until she cried.

"Lucille, I don't know why you not on stage somewhere making some money. Girl you crazy," Mama would always say.

"Good evening."

"Hey Baby," they said in unison.

"How did you do on that test?" Mama asked.

I shrugged. "I won't know until I go back to class on Wednesday."

"Oh, I bet you did fine," Ms. Pearl said as she wiped her eyes on her shirt sleeve.

Mama looked at me carefully before asking, "You hungry? The leftovers from yesterday still in there."

"I had a cheeseburger a while ago. I'm still full from that."

"Well it's wrapped up on a plate in the refrigerator if you get hungry later."

"Thanks Mama. I'm going to take a nap. See you all later."

I dragged myself up the stairs. I dropped my backpack at the foot of the bed and kicked off my shoes before crawling onto the bed. My body welcomed the softness of the mattress. I thought that I would fall asleep in no time at all, but sleep evaded me. I tried counting sheep, but that didn't work. Soon my mind drifted to Rodney and this past weekend.

It was a long time before I finally fell asleep thinking about my conversation with Cynthia. I was jolted awake by the shrill ring of the phone.

I felt as if I had been drugged. "Hello?" I answered groggily.

"Hey Babe, it's me. I wanted to let you know that I got back alright. It was pretty late when I got in, so I didn't want to call then."

Rodney's voice made me remember what I was so angry about before I fell asleep. "Why didn't you tell me that you were still seeing Stacy?"

"What?"

"You heard me. Why didn't you tell me that you were still seeing your old girlfriend? You can have her you know. I won't stand in your way. It's obvious that you still love her."

"Where are you getting all of this nonsense?"

"Well, how did she know that we were no longer together?"

"Hold on Dee-Dee. I did talk to her, but only for a few minutes. I still keep in touch with Kevin. Do you remember him? He's Stacy's brother. We were best friends in school."

"Yes, I remember him."

"The last time I talked to him, I did tell him that we were having some problems and you were back at home, but we were working things out. Stacy was there. I didn't know that at the time. She got on the phone and we talked for a little bit, but that was all Dee-Dee, you gotta believe me."

"Why should I believe you? You lied to me about Teresa and tried to make me think I was losing my mind when I saw the two of you kissing." It didn't take long for the anger to start building up inside of me again.

"Look, I know you don't trust me after that, but I am telling you the truth. Stacy and I have not been seeing each other. For crying out loud, the girl lives in Chicago. How in the world would I see her?"

"The same way you came here, take the bus!"

"I had to save the money to come down there." His voice was rising and I knew it wouldn't be long before this conversation turned ugly.

"You always accuse me of telling people our business, but you see nothing wrong with letting your ex know everything that happens between us."

"She doesn't know everything that happens with us," he yelled. "Why are you trying to make a big deal out of this? I have not seen that girl since she left South Carolina. Whoever told you all of this is trying to make you believe something that's not true Dee-Dee. Who told you this anyway?"

"Suzette told Cynthia when she went to get her hair done. She also said she saw you at the club Saturday night."

"I knew that was coming. Yeah, I did go to the club with a couple of my friends. Why in the world are you listening to Suzette? You know that girl is the biggest gossip in town."

He was clearly upset at this point, and I did not respond.

"Come on Dee, I wasn't with anybody at the club. And if you remember, I wanted us to be together that night. CJ asked me to go with him and some of the guys. He was the one who dropped me off at your job that morning. I said yes just to get out of the house, but nothing happened." He waited for me to say something.

"Are you still there?"

"Yes, I'm here," I said stiffly.

Baby, I didn't call you for all of this. I wanted to let you know that I got back safe and I was going to look for another car next week."

I remained silent as I thought about what he had said.

"Dee-Dee, I promise you I have not seen Stacy since she left and I wasn't with anybody at the club."

Cynthia had already told me that he wasn't with anyone, but I still wasn't sure about him and Stacy. It was hard to believe him after all of his lies about Teresa. "Alright, I heard you!"

"But you don't believe me right? What do I have to do to make you believe me? Do you want Kevin's number so you can call yourself?"

"No, I don't want his number!"

"Then what do you want me to do?"

"Nothing, I just wanted to know why she knew all about our business."

"I told you what I said to Kevin. He obviously told her. But I'm not trying to get back with Stacy. As far as I know, she's got a man."

I could feel the anger beginning to subside a bit.

"You believe me?"

"I guess I'll have to unless I find out something different," I said curtly.

"You won't find out anything different, because there isn't anything to find out," he said clearly annoyed. "Look, I gotta go, the mess hall will be closing in half an hour and I just put my last quarter in the phone. I'll call you again next week."

"Bye."

After we hung up, I thought about our heated discussion and tried to decide whether I believed him or not. It didn't take long for me to start thinking about everything that had happened over the last four days again. I also thought about his sister's comments and decided to give her a call.

I sat up in the bed and dialed the number quickly. I held my breath waiting for her to answer. She picked up on the third ring.

"Jackie here." *What a weird way to answer the phone*, I thought.

"Hey, it's me Claudette."

"Hey. What's up?"

I immediately regretted calling. I didn't know how to start the conversation.

"That peanut head brother of mine isn't causing more trouble, I hope."

I laughed. "I don't think so."

"Did the two of you manage to patch things up?"

I cringed. "Not really."

"Dee-Dee, I like you and I think you're much too nice for my brother. Don't get me wrong. I love my little brother, but I know how he is. He learned all that stuff from Daddy. I can remember when Daddy used to hit Mama and Rodney would get so mad he'd try to run and help her. I had to hold him back. Then as he got older, Daddy started telling him all this stuff about how a man's gotta be a man and show a woman's whose boss and all that other junk. He just started to accept it as normal."

I didn't know what to say, so Jackie went on.

"I know it's kinda hard to resist him. He was always a handsome little kid, but I don't think I'd be lettin' nobody beat on me all the time, I don't care how handsome he is."

"Your mother feels that I should go back to him. She tells me that the Good Book says…"

"We gotta submit to our husbands. Yeah, I know. That's all I heard all my life. Trust me. After witnessing all of that over the years, it has put a bad taste in my mouth about getting married."

I'd often wondered why Jackie wasn't married. She was a beautiful woman. She had her mother's light complexion, but just like Rodney, she had her father's good looks.

"Every time I come close to making that decision; I end up breaking off the relationship. I probably need some counseling or something. She had tried to make it sound like a joke, but I knew she didn't really think it was funny.

"I talked to Rodney about going for counseling."

"Humph, I'm sure that didn't go over well."

"No, it didn't. I really want us to go together, but it's hard to do that with him being in Tennessee."

Jackie gave a short laugh. "Well, I hope that works.

I was silent for a few seconds.

"I don't want to dash your hopes Dee-Dee. I know you love my brother and I wish the two of you well. Counseling sounds like a good idea. I wish Daddy would go too. But that would take a miracle. I'm glad you are considering it though. When Mama told me you had left Rodney, I knew it had to be because he had been hitting you."

I suddenly felt ashamed that she knew about the abuse. I waited for her to go on.

"I just don't want you to end up like my mother. Mama is like a slave in that house. She has no life of her own. Did you ever hear her sing when you stayed there?"

"No."

"Mama has a beautiful voice. She tried several times to join the choir at their church and Daddy always made sure that she never made it to rehearsals or that she couldn't go to church on a regular basis. He tries to kill whatever makes her happy."

It was obvious that Jackie was very angry with her father. "I didn't know that your mother could sing. I heard her humming a few times while I was there."

"I wish you could hear her. She loves to sing, but of course that's something that Daddy can't control, so he doesn't want her doing it. I remember one time she told us about a song she had written when we were kids. I asked her to sing it and she did. It was beautiful. When she was finished, Daddy looked at her and said he had no idea who told her she could sing. I will never forget the look on her face. We never heard her sing again after that."

"I did hear her ask your daddy if the two of them would be going to church a couple times."

"I feel sorry for Mama sometimes and then at other times I get so angry that she keeps letting him get away with treating her that way."

I wondered if Jackie knew that her grandparents had forced their father to marry her mother after he got her pregnant.

"But don't let me tell you what to do. I just wish the two of you well."

"I guess that's why I called because I'm trying to figure out what to do."

"I can't tell you what to do, but if you go back to my brother and he starts hitting you again, you get out of there. I tried to talk to him on the way home on Saturday. I just hope he listened to me."

"Well, thanks for talking to me. I'd better let you go."

"No problem. I'm glad you called. Talk to you later."

Thanks Jackie. I hung up the phone and fell back onto my pillow. Calling Jackie hadn't helped much at all. It only made me more confused about what to do.

Chapter 12

This can't be happening to me. This had to be some kind of mistake. Why now? I knew that Mama was expecting me to come down for breakfast soon, but food was the last thing on my mind. I groaned as I buried my face into my hands. It had been exactly one month since Rodney was here and there was no mistaking what I was experiencing.

"Dee, you 'bout ready to eat?" Mama yelled up to me.

I lifted myself up from the commode and got up to wash my trembling hands before sighing heavily.

"I'm coming." I tried to hide the disappointment that I was feeling from my voice as I made my way down the creaking brown steps. Mama was sitting at the table munching on a big fluffy biscuit.

"I got tired of waitin' on you to let them sheets go and come on down here to eat, so I went on and fixed my plate. Hurry up and fix your food before it gets cold."

I sat down quickly after spooning a dab of eggs on my plate and a slice of bacon. Mama eyed me with her brows raised.

"Chile you feelin' alright? That ain't enough food to feed a bird. You not sick are you?" Mama pushed her chair back and leaned over the table to feel my forehead.

"No Mama. I'm fine. I just had a hard time getting to sleep last night." *Well, at least I didn't lie.* I **had** stayed up for most of the night praying that the tests were wrong and the results would be different if I did it again this morning.

Mama sat down again, but her eyes never left my face. "What's wrong Baby?" Maybe you been workin' too hard Dee-Dee. You might need to slow down." Mama was clearly concerned. She studied me again before munching on a piece of bacon.

"No, that's not it Mama. I just got a lot going on right now, that's all."

"Well no wonder," Mama huffed as she put her fork down. "You takin' all them classes and workin' over time, too."

"I know it's a lot Mama, but I can do it. Don't worry, I'm fine."

"If you say so." Mama put her fork down and looked at me.

I squirmed in the chair as my stomach began to churn wildly. I quickly dabbed at my mouth with a napkin and pushed my chair back. "I'll be right back," I said and ran toward the stairs. As soon as I leaned over the commode, the sour yellow liquid erupted like a volcano as I gagged uncontrollably.

"This is just what I need," I whispered as I cradled the cool porcelain bowl. A few minutes went by before I struggled to stand on my wobbly legs. After washing my face with cold water for the third time this morning, the tumultuous feeling in my stomach began to subside.

Mama was standing over the sink washing the skillet when I came back downstairs. I sat down timidly and stared at the cold, yellow mound in front of me.

Mama turned to look at me and slowly dried her hands on the kitchen towel. She walked over to me and came to stand in front of me. "There somethin' you need to tell me Chile?"

I couldn't bear to look up at Mama as I hung my head and stared at the tan linoleum on the floor.

Mama gently lifted my chin with her finger. I could tell that she knew. I took a deep breath as she moved to sit down in the chair beside me.

I sighed. "I was praying that the result from the test was wrong, so I did it again this morning."

Mama patted my shoulder softly. "Baby, you can't change what's already done."

"This is the last thing I need right now, I said tearfully."

Mama patted my shoulder again. "I know Baby, but God don't make mistakes." The chair squeaked as Mama got up and walked over to the sink. "I know you not too happy 'bout it right now, but it done happen Dee-Dee."

"But what do I do now? Rodney will definitely see this as the chance he's been waiting for to hurry up and get back together."

"When you gonna tell him?"

A feeling of dread gripped my heart. I wasn't ready to tell Rodney that I was pregnant. I still blamed him for causing me to have a miscarriage with my first baby. "I don't know," I whispered. "Ugh! This is hard."

Mama sighed heavily and shook her head. "I know it's gonna be hard, but he got a right to know Baby."

"I just need some time to think about all this. I don't want to raise a baby alone."

Mama dried her hands again and turned to face me. "Just take one day at a time Baby."

I thought about my choices. If I didn't go back to Rodney, I would be like Sharon. Somehow I couldn't see myself as a single parent. Children needed both of their parents. I remembered how hard Mama had to struggle after Daddy died. I couldn't do that to my baby. I thought about going to see Pastor West again, but quickly decided against that idea. But maybe he would really try to make our marriage work now that we had a baby on the way. *I had to give him a chance.* It would be hard to leave Mama again, but I had to try one more time to make my marriage work, for the sake of my unborn child.

I jumped when the phone rang. The long green cord tangled immediately when Mama picked up the receiver from the wall.

"Hello," she said briskly. "Hey Pearl. No, I don't think it come yet." Mama leaned her elbows on the counter as she listened to the voice on the other end. "You know how Lucille is. She wants to get it cheap as possible."

I got up and quickly scraped the hardened food from my plate trying not to listen to Mama's conversation. I washed the plate, let the water out of the sink, and dried my hands before heading toward the stairs. Mama dragged the old wooden chair to the counter so that she could sit down while she talked to Miss. Pearl.

Two hours later, my room was spotless, but it didn't help me forget about the situation in which I now found myself. Rodney was planning to come home for Christmas in a little less than a month. *What would he say when he found out that I was pregnant?* He would definitely want me to give up on my dreams of getting my college degree. *Maybe I shouldn't tell him.* But he was sure to find out eventually. This was his mother's fault. If she hadn't tricked me into coming over there that day, this wouldn't have happened.

I was not as excited about this pregnancy like I was with the first one. *This is just not a good time for us to be having a baby.* There was no one that I could talk to about this. The only one I would want to talk to about it was Francine and I hadn't talked to her in weeks. I was too embarrassed to tell her what had happened when

Rodney came home last month. What would she think of me if I went back to Rodney? *No, I can't tell her right now.* My stomach was in knots as I thought about my options.

A few hours later, I quietly made my way to the kitchen to keep from disturbing Mama's nap. As thoughtful as ever, she had covered the biscuits and left them on the counter for me. It took no time at all to fix a quick meal of biscuits with butter and honey. Thankfully, today was my day off, so I could spend the rest of the day trying to figure this out.

Everything was happening so fast. In a little over a month, it was possible that we would be living together again. *Could it be different this time?* The nagging doubts lingered. We had a baby on the way that would need a father and a mother. I really didn't want to get back together with Rodney without going to counseling. *That's it! I'll make an appointment for us to meet with the pastor.*

As my mind drifted back to my pregnancy, I wondered about the baby that I lost in April. Was it a boy or girl? I should be thrilled to be pregnant again, but I wasn't. Our baby deserved to be raised in a loving home like the one I had grown up in. My parents loved each other and they weren't afraid to let everyone around them know that. Daddy went out of his way to make Mama happy. Because of their love for each other, I never doubted how much they loved me. Why didn't I marry someone more like Daddy? How could I have been so wrong about Rodney?

The year that I met Rodney was a very difficult one for me. I had been so unsure of myself. I wasn't very outgoing and tended to shy away from sports and other school related activities. Rodney came into my life during a time when I was extremely vulnerable. I remember missing Daddy terribly that year and having a lot of questions about boys. If only he could have been there for me to talk to.

Rodney was so handsome and sure of himself. Girls practically threw themselves at him, so I couldn't believe that he could be interested in me. There were many guys trying to talk to me, but I was very withdrawn. Rodney's outgoing personality is what drew me to him at first. I wanted to be that way, but I wasn't sure how to do it. My self esteem was pretty low at the time too. There was no doubt that Mama loved me, but I wanted something more. I needed my daddy and for some strange reason, Rodney seemed to fill that void.

Mama never cared for Rodney. When I brought him home to meet her, we sat across from her in the living room and fidgeted nervously on the faded crème sofa as we waited for her first words. Mama began by asking Rodney a laundry list of questions. She appeared to be looking into his very soul. I could tell by the look on her face that day that she did not approve of my decision.

Rodney kept glancing in my direction every time Mama asked a question. His eyes pleaded with me as if I could magically fix the situation. I was her only child. Her little miracle, she always told me and she didn't feel that Rodney was best for me.

"Your daddy and me had given up on ever having a child of our own," she told me once when I asked why I had no brothers or sisters. "We tried for years to have a baby, but nothin' happened. When we found out I was pregnant, your daddy was the happiest man alive. Lawd Chile, I thought I'd have to tie that man down the way he danced all around this house. You were the prettiest baby alive. Your daddy named you, Claudette Olivia Chapman after his mama"

"Who started calling me Dee-Dee?"

"I guess we both did. You were as cute as a button and such a tiny little thing. Claudette seemed like a big name for such a tiny little baby."

I closed my eyes and smiled and tried to picture my daddy dancing around the house. I can't ever remember seeing my daddy without a smile on his face. He used to play tricks on my mama all the time to get her to smile.

I knew she wanted what was best for me, but I just wanted her to give Rodney a chance. The tone of voice she used to question him made it pretty clear that she had made her decision about Rodney and it wasn't good.

"So what are your plans for the future young man?"

"I'm just waiting for the recruiter to contact me and let me know what I need to do next," Rodney said.

"I see." Mama studied Rodney's face as she sized him up. He squirmed beside me on the sofa and tried to regain his composure. He was about to say something when she asked, "So what are your intentions toward my daughter?"

The question shocked me.

"Uh, I…" Rodney glanced in my direction again silently begging for my help. "Uh, we are just going together right now, Ms.

Chapman."

"What happens when things start to get serious?"

"Mama we both got our own goals," I said, trying to take some of the pressure off Rodney.

He smiled at me.

"I am still planning to go to nursing school and become a RN."

"And how do you feel about that young man?" I noticed that mama never called Rodney by his name.

"Well, uh, we never talked about it."

I frowned. Rodney had never asked me what my plans were after graduation. We had a month left in school and had only talked about his plans and his dreams.

Mama got up slowly from the table and turned to go upstairs to her bedroom. "Dee-Dee, I'll excuse myself now. Don't forget to turn off the lights when your guest leaves. Goodnight young man."

"Goodnight," Rodney squeaked.

I knew that her door would remain open so that she could hear what went on downstairs. Rodney and I sat there for a few minutes listening to her as she slowly made her way up the stairs. The steps creaked under the pressure of her weight.

"So what's up with your mom? She doesn't like me," Rodney whispered.

I motioned for him to join me on the porch. After closing the door behind me, I turned to him and shrugged my shoulders. "She's just trying to protect me. You know how parents are?"

"Well, I gotta go. I need to pick up something for my mom from the store."

"Wait a minute. I need to ask you something before you go. Why haven't you ever asked me about what I plan to do after graduation?"

Rodney tried to smile but it seemed more like a smirk to me. "It just never came up."

"But we talk about what you're going to do all the time and you never ask me about my goals."

Rodney started fidgeting once more.

"Look it's no big deal, OK. I just didn't think about it. I'm sorry, but in my family women don't work. They stay home and take care of the house. I would be making enough money so you would never have to work. You could take care of the house and the kids, and look pretty for me when I come home."

I sucked in my breath and held it just in case somebody tried to change what had just taken place. Was that a proposal? Did Rodney Jackson just ask me to marry him? He held my face in his hands and held my eyes with his. He had a weird smirk on his face before he kissed me.

"So do you think your mama would let you marry me?"

I felt as if I was going to pass out. I couldn't believe my ears. Rodney Jackson was really talking about marriage and we weren't even out of high school yet.

"Well, I don't know. We would have to ask her."

"And what if she says no?"

I didn't know how to respond

"Would you still marry me if she said no?" Rodney asked as he pulled me toward him.

With Rodney so close, and staring down at me, I knew there was no way I could say, no. I nodded my head.

"Then let's seal that nod with a kiss."

As soon as Rodney's car backed out of my yard, I ran to the phone to call Cynthia.

"Girl, you are not going to believe what just happened!" I blurted into the phone as soon as she answered.

"What?"

I screamed with my fist against my mouth.

"What happened girl?"

I could hear the impatience in her voice as I tried to calm down, but I wanted to keep Cynthia hanging for as long as possible.

"Rodney just asked me to marry him," I blurted.

"What! Are you putting me on?"

I could hear her scream on the other end of the phone. "Well, what did you say?"

"What do you mean what did I say? I told him, yes."

I laughed as I heard her scream again.

"But what will your mama say?" I could hear the apprehension in her voice. She knew how much my mother wanted me to go to college and get my nursing degree.

"Well, that's going to be the tough part. I don't think mama likes Rodney."

"Then you'd better wait until she's in a good mood to break the news to her about this proposal."

"I don't know if there will be a day when she's in a good mood. She's been in a lot of pain lately. I hear her walking the floors at night."

"Is it the arthritis again?"

"Yeah and I think her blood pressure is up again too."

"Well you have to tell her sometime."

"Yeah I know, but there's more. Rodney says that he doesn't want me to work. He says he'll be making enough money so I won't have to work. I can just stay home and take care of the kids."

Cynthia whistled softly into the phone. There was silence on the other end of the phone for a few seconds. "I don't know Dee. That sounds good, but what if something happens between the two of you? At least you would always have your nursing degree."

"What do you mean if something happens? Nothing's going to happen with us," I protested.

"I know, but why don't you wait until after college to get married. Then you could stay home and still have your degree just in case."

I thought about what she had said. It made sense to me. I just didn't know how Rodney was going to take it. "I'll run that one by him and see what he says."

"What do you mean, see what he says? It's your decision too?" Cynthia must have known that her last comment didn't go over well when I didn't answer her after a few seconds.

"OK, let's not get into that. I know you all happy and everything and I don't want to mess that up. Congratulations girl."

"Thanks, I wanted to call and let you know. I gotta go."

After I hung up the phone, I sat there for a few minutes thinking about Cynthia's question. Why was I leaving the decision up to Rodney? Wasn't it my life too?

Now, over a year later, I still found myself forced to deal with some of the very issues that had been ignored in the beginning. Why had I given up on my dream so easily? I didn't have long to think before the phone rang. I answered it quickly before it could ring a second time.

"Hello."

"Hey it's me. I got good news."

"What?"

"We got quarters. It'll be ready in three weeks. They need to do a little bit of work to it, but we got a place in Lee Village."

I did not welcome Rodney's news. Getting a place on post was what I dreamed about when we were together, but now all I could think of was that he had already made up his mind that we were getting back together and he wasn't interested in what I had to say at all. And now here I was pregnant. Rodney went on without waiting for my reply.

"When I come to get you, we'll go and sell your car so that we won't have to drive two cars back up here."

Sell my car! That got my attention. "Sell my car? I don't want to sell my car."

"Why do we need two cars? Dee we can use one car like we did before. We won't have to pay out extra money to keep car insurance on two cars."

The last time we talked he told me that he had finally saved enough money to get another car. But I loved my little car!

"Dee?"

"I heard you. I was just thinking that's all."

"I should be there a couple days before Christmas." Rodney went on as if it was all settled. He didn't bother to wait for me to respond. "We'll stay until the day after Christmas and come back up here. I thought I was going to be able to leave a week before the holidays, but the commander wouldn't sign off on it. I can't wait to see you."

The only thing that was on my mind right now was this baby that I was carrying. I didn't have the energy to fight with Rodney right now, so I just listened. It was hard keeping the pregnancy from Rodney, but I just didn't want to tell him right now.

"Hey, I can't wait for you to see the place Dee. It's much bigger than our last one."

It was obvious that Rodney was excited about us getting the apartment on post. A year ago, I would have been just as happy.

"What's wrong Dee?"

"Nothing's wrong. Why?"

"You just seem so quiet."

"I would like for us to start going to counseling together Rodney." *Now where did that come from?* I hadn't planned to say that to him. There was silence on the other end, so I held my breath.

"Why you keep going back to the past Dee-Dee? Are you looking for something to pick a fight about?"

"No, I'm not looking for a reason to pick a fight," I said calmly. "I need you to understand that if we get back together, we are going to need some help. I want us to start going to counseling or I'm not coming up there." I was surprised by how calm I had been and so matter-of- fact.

There was a long moment of silence on the other end. "Fine, if that's what you want, we'll go to counseling. I don't see what good it's going to do. We'll be paying out money for something we can handle on our own. But if that's what you want, fine."

I knew this was going to be an uphill battle, but right now I didn't have a choice. I knew I wanted to give it one more chance for the sake of our baby.

"Hey, I gotta go. I need to take the car in and get a tune up so it'll be ready for the road. I'll talk to Daddy and see if he can find somebody to buy your car."

I didn't trust myself to speak

"I'll talk to you later, bye."

So it had all been settled. He was continuing to make plans for us to be together in spite of everything that I had said to him, but at least he had agreed to counseling, that was a step in the right direction. Why wasn't I thrilled about this small victory?

Chapter 13

I sighed heavily and got out of the bed. I waited to see if the familiar feeling of nausea would come, but it didn't. Morning sickness was the last thing I needed right now. I only had an hour and thirty minutes before I needed to be at work.

"They say every pregnancy is different. Some women get sick all the time with one and not at all with the other," Mama replied when I told her I wasn't getting sick every morning as I had with the first pregnancy.

Surprisingly, Mama was dressed and sitting on the sofa when I got downstairs. She smiled when she saw the expression on my face.

"Good Morning Mama."

"Mornin' Baby, I'm waitin' on Lucille. We goin' downtown early so we can get back here before the soaps come on."

I smiled and shook my head. Mama and her friends hated to miss their soaps. It started with The Young and the Restless and ended with General Hospital. Thankfully, I wasn't one for watching much TV or I would be waiting in front of the television the way they did on a daily basis.

"Try to eat somethin' before you go to work Dee-Dee."

I knew that Mama was concerned about how little I was eating lately, but I hated to be nauseous and I thought that not eating a lot would help.

"I'll just grab a piece of toast and some juice. I don't have a lot of time."

"Baby you need to eat a full breakfast. That baby need nourishment."

There was no point in arguing with Mama. She would watch me like a hawk to make sure I ate something before leaving the house. *What was quick and easy*? I poured myself a small bowl of cereal and sat down at the table.

"Did you two decide on a date yet?"

Before I could answer a drizzle of milk ran down my chin. I quickly reached over to grab a napkin before answering. Thinking about the day when I would be moving back to Tennessee was my least favorite topic right now, but Mama deserved to know what my plans were.

"Rodney won't be able to come when he had planned. He has duty and no one wanted to switch with him, so it looks like he'll get here on Monday." Mama took a few minutes before responding.

"You tell him yet?"

I dreaded the question. *What was keeping me from telling him that we were going to have a baby?* "Not yet. I'll just wait until he comes and tell him then."

Mama looked at me and nodded. Her eyes clearly said that she knew there was more to the story than I was willing to share, but she didn't press the issue.

"I wonder what's keeping Lucille. She usually at the door knockin' before I can finish gettin' dressed good."

Mama was right. It wasn't like Ms. Lucille to be late.

She looked at her watch again and frowned. "I wonder if she got sick again. She said she wasn't feelin' good yesterday."

"You want me to run over there and check on her?" I quickly pushed my chair back and poured the rest of the cereal in the sink and rinsed it out quickly.

"I don't want to make you late for work. I'll walk over there if she don't get here in the next few minutes. Her old bones might be actin' up again and it just takes some time to get things going that's all."

"Are you sure Mama? It won't take but a few minutes to go over there."

Mama looked down at her watch again and nodded. "OK, just see what's keepin' her. I'll wait at the door so you won't have to come all the way back."

I grabbed my purse and gulped down some juice. "I'll see you later Mama." I reached down to give her a quick peck on the top of her head as I walked to the door.

When I got to Ms. Lucille's house, I knocked several times and waited for her to come to the door. After a few minutes, I looked back at our house and I could see Mama standing in the door. I shrugged to let her know that I didn't hear anything inside. I tried knocking several more times and got no response. I peeked through the tiny slit of glass in the front door, but I couldn't see past one section of the living room. When I turned back to look at Mama, she was already making her way across the street to join me. Mama was hurrying as best she could and I knew it would take her a few minutes. I thought about running back to my car and driving the short distance to pick her up.

Mama fumbled with her keys when she got up on the steps. She was out of breath and I could see her hands shaking. "Now which one of these is Lucille's key? Here, Baby, try this one."

The key didn't fit. Mama took them out of my hand. "That one must be Pearl's. Here try this one."

I tried the second key and jiggled it around in the lock before it unlocked the door. Mama pushed past me and immediately started calling for her friend.

"Lucille, what's takin' you old woman? You forgot we supposed to be goin' to King Street today?"

I waited by the door. It felt funny being in someone else's house when they hadn't invited you in. I knew it was OK for Mama. They had keys to each other's homes in case of emergency. Mama walked toward the back of the house and I heard her knock sharply on a door.

"You in here Lucille?"

I looked down at my watch. I had twenty minutes to get to work and that was pushing it. I heard Mama scream before I could look up.

"Oh Lawd no!"

I ran into the house and raced to the back room. Mama was shaking the stiff body of the woman who had been her friend since childhood.

Three hours later, I sat at the kitchen table with Mama and Ms. Pearl. The undertaker had taken the body away and the fact that their friend was gone was finally beginning to sink in. I had called in to say that I had a family emergency and couldn't come in. There was no way that I could leave Mama right now.

I had fixed them several cups of tea and tried to get them to eat, but they refused. They were grief stricken and I felt helpless. Ms. Pearl had gone through an entire box of Kleenex and tears were still cascading down her cheeks. Mama seemed withdrawn and lost in her thoughts. It was hard to know what to do to help them.

"Mama, I'm going for a drive. Do you need anything before I go?

"No. You go on. We'll be alright."

Ms. Pearl nodded before dabbing at her puffy, red eyes. "Yeah, you go on Dee-Dee."

I glanced back at them quickly before leaving. I had no idea where I was going, but it was too hard sitting there watching the two of them. Feelings of sadness began to wash over me as I thought back to the days after Daddy died. I didn't know what to do with myself then either. I would always go outside to find my friends hoping that being with them would take my mind off the grief I didn't know how to express.

After driving around the block a few times, I headed toward Hampton Park. I parked and sat there for awhile thinking about the day that Rodney and I had come here right before he left for Boot Camp. It seemed like such a long time ago. We had made plans for our future as we tried to make every second count before going through the long months of separation.

A family of four parked beside me. The children, a little boy and a girl, squealed loudly in the backseat. I watched them as they unpacked their things and walked to the grassy area. The woman looked to be a few years older than me. She was short and round. The kids skipped around happily as she spread a blanket on the ground and the man began tossing a large ball up and down. The children giggled and ran around in circles.

It was hard to keep from smiling as I watched them prepare for their picnic in the park, but it made me sad to think that things were so uncertain for Rodney and me. Watching them increased my anxieties about my own family. I decided to go somewhere else.

I drove around for a bit and ended up on Popular Street. Cynthia lived on this street now. I wondered if she was home. I parked in front of her house and sat there debating with myself about whether or not I should try to make amends. After a few minutes, I got out of the car and walked to the door. I checked my watch. It was still early. I grimaced before tapping on the door lightly. *She's probably still asleep, knowing her.*

I tried to think of what I was going to say to her. I didn't have long to think before the door opened.

"Dee-Dee, what are you doing here?"

I didn't detect any anger in her voice, just surprise. "I was just driving around. I know it's early, but I took a chance on coming by anyway."

"Come on in. I just finished getting my list together before I go to the grocery store. I need to pick up a few things before my first customer comes."

I stepped into the apartment and stood in the doorway directly in front of the steps that lead upstairs. I glanced around quickly.

"Why don't I come with you and we can talk on the way."

"Fine with me, let me get my purse." Cynthia walked over to the kitchen table and grabbed a large black and white stripped purse from the table.

"You still like carrying a suitcase for a purse, I see."

Cynthia gave me a short laugh. "And I still need more room for all the extra junk I try to pack in it."

"Why don't I drive? I'm probably blocking you in anyway."

She shrugged. "If you want to, it doesn't matter to me. I just need to get a few things for the shop and a couple things from Winn-Dixie."

We got in the car and I carefully pulled away from the curb.

"This is a cute car. This is the first time I've been in here."

"Thanks."

We were both silent as we headed to the store. I couldn't think of how I wanted to start the conversation about our last phone call.

"So how are things going for you at school?" Cynthia asked lightly. It was obvious that she was having a hard time coming up with something to say too. This was strange. Cynthia and I had never had an argument before. Well, not as adults anyway. We argued all the time when we were kids, but it was all over by the next day and we played together like nothing had happened. It was different now and we both knew it.

"Things are going good. The semester will end in a couple weeks."

"That's good. You were always smart with the books. I'm sure you will do fine."

"Ms. Lucille died this morning."

Cynthia turned to me quickly. "What! Was she sick or something?"

"No. We found her this morning. She died in her sleep."

"Oh man. I know it must be hard on your mom and Ms. Pearl. How they takin' it?"

"It's been hard. That was one of the reasons I had to get out this morning. It's tough seeing them so torn up about it. It reminds of how things were when Daddy died."

"I'm sorry Dee-Dee." She was silent for a few seconds before adding. "I'll have to call my mom when I get back home and tell her. She'll want to bring something by and sit with them for awhile. Do they know when they will try to have the funeral?"

"No. Mama and Ms. Pearl called her family as soon as they could. They will probably decide all that when they get here. Most of her family is in New York. I haven't seen any of them in years and probably wouldn't recognize them if I saw them."

"Man, this is sad to hear. I remember how she used to get on to us all the time for running through her little flower garden." Cynthia laughed. "She didn't have but two or three little flowers."

I smiled. "Yeah, I remember that. But **you** were the one trampling all over her flowers, not me."

"Oh please. You were right there with me."

We drove along silently for a few minutes before I worked up the nerve to tell her why I had come by. "I wanted to apologize for hanging up on you and getting all upset the other day."

"I'm sorry too. I should have told you when Suzette told me about it. I guess I was trying to get back at you for not telling me in the first place."

"I know. I was embarrassed."

We talked for the rest of the trip. When we got back to her house, we sat in the car to finish the conversation. By the time I left her house, I had pretty much told her all that had happened when I moved away to Tennessee. There were times when she was so mad, that I could see the nerves twitching in her jaw.

"So what are you going to do now? I know you don't want to raise the baby alone, but women do it all the time."

"I just don't want my baby to grow up without a father. I wished my daddy could have been there for me."

"Dee, I know it will be hard, but you can't let this guy keep hitting you. I mean what if he really hurt you the next time."

I was silent as I thought about her question. "I know, that's why I want us to go to counseling together, but it's hard to do if we are apart."

Cynthia shook her head. "I suggest knocking him out with a frying pan if he tries to hit you again. He has to go to sleep some time."

100

We both laughed. "I don't want there to be a next time, that's why we need to get some help."

Cynthia glanced at her watch. "I gotta go. I'll call you later to finish our conversation. It was like old times again."

"Yeah, it was," I replied.

"I want to be there for the funeral. Make sure you let me know when it's going to be." She grabbed her packages and got out of the car. She waved and quickly made her way to her door.

I beeped the horn and headed back home. Hopefully Mama would be ready to eat something. I definitely didn't want her to get sick over all of this.

When I walked in the door, I didn't see Mama sitting in her rocking chair. Everything was quiet. I went upstairs and tapped lightly on her bedroom door.

"Mama, do you need anything?"

"No. I just want to rest for awhile," she answered gruffly.

She had obviously been crying. I tiptoed to my room and shut the door behind me. I lay across the bed and thought about everything that had happened today and picked up the phone to call Francine. I knew that it was going to be hard to tell her about all that happened since we last talked. I had missed her call several times and had made no attempt to call her back.

The phone rang twice before Francine picked up. "Hello."

"Francine, it's me."

"Hey. It's been a long time since I heard from you. How you doing?"

"I'm fine. Mama told me you called a couple times. I'm sorry I'm just now getting back to you."

"So what's been going on with you?"

I hesitated before responding to her question. "So much has happened that I don't even know where to begin."

"What happened? You don't sound like yourself."

The concern in her voice brought tears to my eyes. When I finished, Francine whistled softly into the phone.

"Claudette, I know this must be hard for you. I can't imagine what you must be going through."

"I just need to know that I'll be making the right decision if I go back to Rodney," I said.

"I don't know how you could know that for sure. That would be a chance you would be taking. Nobody can tell you what to do. Just take your time and think through this, Claudette. I agree that your baby needs a father, but that baby will need to be raised in a loving environment too."

I sighed heavily. "Yeah, I know."

"Claudette, I have to go. I need to get to a meeting at the church. I'm glad we had the chance to talk. I'll be praying for you, girl."

"Thanks," I whispered. "Take care and I'll talk to you later," I said before hanging up.

I thought about my conversation with Francine for a long time before finally drifting off to sleep.

❧ *Chapter 14* ❦

The service for Ms. Lucille was heartbreaking. Mama and Ms. Pearl tried to comfort each other as best they could in the days leading up to the funeral, but watching the two of them as they hovered over the casket was unbearable. I had gone through two handkerchiefs and a handful of tissue.

Most of Ms. Lucille's relatives had come, so the tiny church was jam packed and people were forced to stand along the wall. Her only son stood hunched over on a cane as he waited his turn to be ushered past his mother's body. In all the years that I had known Ms. Lucille I had never seen her son. Mama said he was injured in Vietnam and it was hard for him to get around. Ms. Lucille used to take trips to Maryland every now and then to see him, but it had been difficult for her to do that lately. The other relatives that came in from New York had looked to Mama and Ms. Pearl for help in organizing the funeral.

It was good that Mama and Ms. Pearl had something to do to keep them busy. Mama hadn't been herself since the day we found Ms. Lucille dead in her room. The results of the autopsy would be weeks away, but the coroner said he believed she had died naturally.

"I'm just glad she was asleep," Ms. Pearl sobbed as she sat with Mama at the kitchen table last night. She probably didn't feel a thing."

Mama nodded and sipped her coffee. "I still can't believe she gone Pearl," she said forlornly.

It was hard seeing my mother this way. I just wanted to wrap my arms around her and tell her how much I loved her. I jumped when a lady in front of me wailed mournfully. Those around her tried to restrain her, but it wasn't working. The ushers ran over with a handful of fans.

"My auntie gone," she wailed over and over until someone sitting next to her whispered softly in her ear to calm her. I was sitting on the last row of the tiny church because I had gotten off from work late.

By the time I hurried home to get dressed, it was too late to join Mama and Ms. Pearl in the processional. They were sitting near the front of the church with the family. The two of them had been like sisters to Ms. Lucille and it was fitting for them to be included in the family's decisions. In a way, I was glad that I had to work today. It had helped to keep my mind off the funeral for a little while.

Cynthia had kept her word and was sitting with her mother a few rows in front of me. She escorted her mother down the aisle after viewing the body and waved to me when she walked by.

I had decided early on not to view the body. It was just too much for me to handle right now. Mama saw me as she walked slowly past my row with Ms. Pearl. She reached out to me for me to join them. I quickly grabbed my purse and squeezed past the people standing on either side of me.

"When I didn't see you, I wondered if you had made it at all," Mama whispered when I got close to her. "You didn't want to sit up front with us?"

"I got here late," I said quietly as we made our way out of the church. All three of us pulled our coats tightly around us when we walked out of the church and into the chilly December afternoon.

Mama rode with me to the burial site on James Island. I wished that I could have stayed in the car and watched from a distance, but she wanted me with her. Graveyards always gave me the creeps. As the minister gave the last words, I thought about Daddy's funeral. It seemed weird that I couldn't remember much about Daddy's burial site and a lot of the procedures seemed very foreign to me.

I was thankful when it was all over so that I could escape to my room. I left Mama and Ms. Pearl in the kitchen as they relived the day's events. I tried to block it all out as I thought about Rodney and our baby. I was having an even harder time getting used to the idea that I could be moving back to Tennessee soon and leaving Mama alone so soon after Ms. Lucille's death. It didn't seem right to leave her now. *Maybe I should stay until after the New Year.*

As I thought about Mama, it suddenly came to me that it would be a good idea to leave my car with her and Ms. Pearl. Rodney had suggested that I sell it the last time we talked, but the two women would need transportation now that their friend was gone. Ms. Lucille had taken on the role of being the chauffeur for her two friends and happily took them wherever they needed to go. One of her family members had laid claim to her car and would be driving it back to New York tomorrow morning. The car Ms. Pearl had wasn't working and Mama had never had a license. If I left my car, the two women would be able to get around. The plan sounded good to me.

I looked at my watch and put the phone beside me. Rodney had said he would call today around 5:00. It was already six o'clock. *What was taking him so long?* My stomach growled loudly as I thought about going downstairs to fix a sandwich. Before I could get up, the phone rang beside me.

"Hello."

"Hey, it's me. How was the funeral?"

"It was sad. It reminded me of when Daddy died. I was glad when it was over."

"That must have been hard," he said after several seconds.

"Yeah."

"Give your mom my condolences."

"I will."

"Not to change subject, but I got my leave approved, so I'll be there Monday afternoon around six."

I didn't respond.

"Did you hear me? I'll be there on Monday," he repeated.

"Yeah I heard you. I was just wondering if it's a good time to leave Mama."

"What do you mean?" Rodney sounded confused.

"Her best friend just died. It's not a good time to leave her right now that's all." I held my breath as I waited for him to respond.

"Babe, we already made plans. I know it's tough on her losing her friend, but I already signed for the place."

"I know, but what difference will another few weeks make. Can't we just wait until after the new year?"

"So is that what this is all about? You want to be there for the holidays," he asked irritably. "We haven't seen each other in months. Seem like you would want to bring in the new year with your husband."

Here we go again, I thought. Everything always had to be about him. "I do want to see you, but Mama needs me right now," I whined.

"I need you too, Dee-Dee. You've been there for six months now. I want us to be back together again."

I didn't know what to say, so I didn't say anything.

"So what, you don't want me to come?"

I didn't want to tell him, but that was exactly what I was hoping for. "I just want to be there for Mama. She's always been there for me," I snapped.

"Dee-Dee, I'm not going to be able to take time off again for awhile. I need to get you all moved in.

It was hard to think of a response. Things were moving too fast.

I want us to be able to spend some time together. Why can't you understand that?" The exasperation was clear in his voice.

"I do understand."

"It's not like your mom will be alone. Ms. Pearl is still there. Come on Dee-Dee. I already put in my leave and everything."

I refused to answer.

"Dee, are you still there?"

"I'm here. I'm still thinking about it. And I don't want to sell my car. I'm going to leave it for Mama and Ms. Pearl so that they will be able to get around. Now that Ms. Lucille is gone, they will need some transportation."

"Dee-Dee your mama doesn't have a license," he replied sarcastically.

"I know that, but Ms. Pearl has one and she will be able to get Mama around just like Ms. Lucille used to do."

Rodney sighed loudly. "I thought we had agreed to use the money we made on the car to get some new furniture?"

"I know, but this is more important. I don't want Mama to have to worry about taking the city bus at her age."

"They can use Ms. Pearl's car."

"It's not running right now."

"It's your car. You can do whatever you want with it," he snapped.

"I think it's best to leave the car with them!"

"This was probably not the best day to call you. I'll see you on Monday. I gotta go. Later."

He hung up before giving me a chance to say goodbye.

I sighed heavily before hanging up the phone. He was obviously not going to change his plans about coming home next week, but at least I would be able to leave my car for Mama.

I went downstairs a few minutes later to get something to eat. Mama was sitting alone in the living room looking at Daddy's picture.

"Hey Mama."

"Hey Baby. Did you get some rest?"

"I wasn't sleeping. I was on the phone with Rodney." I glanced over at her to see her reaction.

"Oh…and how he doin," she replied before looking back at the picture.

"Fine, he'll be here Monday.

"I see."

I told him I wanted to stay for another couple of weeks. I don't want to leave you alone right now."

Mama looked up at me quickly. "No, Baby. You go on wid your husband. I'll be alright."

I kneeled down beside her. "You sure Mama?

"Yes, I'm sure."

I just don't want to leave you alone so soon after…."

Mama patted my head and smiled. "I appreciate you thinkin' about me, but your mama will be just fine."

I sighed. "Well, I am leaving the car with Ms. Pearl. I don't want you to have to worry about taking the bus anywhere," I said adamantly.

Mama laughed. "What you tryin' to say? You think I done got too old to take the bus?" She laughed and shook her head.

I got up and sat beside her on the sofa. "No, I don't think you're too old. I just want you and Ms. Pearl to be able to get around when you need to, that's all."

"And what did Rodney think about that?"

"He said it was my car and I could do what I wanted with it." Of course the way he said it was a bit harsher, but I knew Mama was watching me carefully, so I tried to make my voice light.

"Baby, I been gettin' round long before you were born. I know you just want to look out for your mama, but don't worry 'bout me Dee-Dee. I'll be fine."

I shook my head. "I'm leaving the car Mama. It will make me feel better to know that you have something to get around in."

"Dee-Dee, that car is yours."

"Please Mama."

"Alright, if you insist, go ahead and leave the car. Pearl can drive it. It'll be the first time in a long time she won't have to drive an old beat up car. She'll get a kick outta that."

I laughed lightly. "I'm sure she will."

Mama smiled.

It made me feel a little better to see her smile. Leaving the car for them was the right thing to do.

❧ Chapter 15 ❧

Rodney was coming today and I was a nervous wreck. Where had the time gone? There were only five days left before Christmas. *Lord, please let this plan work.* He was going to be angry when he found out what I had done, but he had left me no choice. I told him that I would meet him at his mother's house when I got off from work.

I glanced in the mirror one last time and checked my watch. He should be there by now. It was almost time to go. My hands were sweaty and my heart raced as I thought about what I was about to do. I hurried downstairs, thankful that Mama was visiting with Ms. Pearl and wasn't there to ask a lot of question. I hadn't told her of my plan because I didn't want her to talk me out of it.

I carefully backed the car out of the driveway and headed toward his parents house. *What was he going to say when he found out what I had done?* I shuddered, but nothing was going to stop me now. I sighed a deep sigh of relief when I spotted Jackie's little car parked in the yard. There was another car there that I hadn't seen before, so I assumed it must be Rodney's. He must have been looking for me, because he walked out of the house as soon as I got out of the car. He smiled and quickly came to stand beside me.

"Hey," he said before pulling me toward him for a kiss.

"Why don't you two get a motel," Jackie said when she walked out of the house.

Rodney sighed and took a deep breath before pulling away from me and leaning against the car. "Don't you have somewhere to be?" he snarled.

Jackie ignored him. "So what's going on Dee-Dee? How is school?"

"It's fine." We talked for a few minutes about school before Rodney piped in.

"You come to see me or my sister?"

"Oh be quiet brat!"

"Who you calling a brat?"

"You! What's wrong with me talking to Dee-Dee? You'll have her all to yourself later on." Jackie rolled her eyes at him and continued talking to me.

Rodney walked away angrily. "Don't let me stop the two of you. Let me know when you're through." He went to sit on the porch and glared at us angrily.

"Don't pay him no mind," Jackie whispered. "He's always been a pain in the butt."

The two of us continued talking before we were interrupted by Mrs. Jackson.

"Hello, Dee-Dee. I didn't know you were here." She looked at Rodney quickly and I thought I saw a slight smile on her face before she nodded her head to show her approval. "It's good to see the two of you workin' things out."

I looked at Jackie in time to see her roll her eyes before shaking her head.

"You had lunch yet Dee-Dee? I can warm up something if you hungry."

"No thank you. I ate already."

"Well alright. I'll leave ya'll young people alone. Jacqueline, I got a pie I want you to take to Ms. Ella down the street. She's been sick. Rodney come and get this pie for me."

Jackie groaned as she rolled her eyes again.

Mrs. Jackson went back into the house. Rodney got up reluctantly and followed his mother into the house.

"So you sure this is going to work?" Jackie asked as soon as he went in the house.

"I don't know, but I sure hope so."

"How are you going to get him to go in?"

I shrugged. "I don't know yet. I'll think of something."

We stopped talking as soon as we heard the door open. I glanced at Jackie and waited for her cue.

She turned to look at Rodney and smiled. So little brother, why don't you take us for a ride in your new car?"

Rodney was not amused. He gave her a hard look before responding. "It's not new. It's four years old," he snapped.

Jackie was not put off by his coldness. "It looks new to me and I'm sure it runs better than mine. She walked toward his car and started looking in the window. "It even smells new."

"Yeah, why don't you take us for a ride?" I could tell that he was surprised that I wanted to go for a ride too.

He looked at me and then nodded. "OK, let's go."

110

Jackie looked at me and winked before getting in the backseat. "We can drop the pie off on the way."

Rodney looked at me again before turning toward the car. I quickly slid into the front seat and waited for him to get in. It didn't take long for the aroma of the hot apple pie to fill the car.

"Whoever owned this car kept it up well, Jackie said over my shoulders. It's nice. I might have to get me a Camaro now. I like it."

After we dropped off the pie to Ms. Ella, we were on our way.

"So where do you two want to go," Rodney asked turning to look at me.

"Just keep straight and go on out toward the Interstate," Jackie said.

Rodney frowned, but he kept going.

I could feel the tremors in my stomach as we neared the exit for the church.

"Could we turn off at the next exit? I just remembered that I need to make a quick stop by the church."

Rodney glanced at me quickly. "What you need to go to the church for at this time of the day? Won't it be closed?"

I want to say goodbye to Pastor. I won't see him again before we leave." Rodney was bound to be suspicious, but it was the best answer I could think of.

Rodney took the exit and waited for me to tell him where to go. Five minutes later we were in the parking lot.

God, I need help. "Why don't you come in with me and meet Pastor West. I'm sure he will be happy to see you," I said brightly.

"No, I'll wait here." He turned off the ignition and settled back in the seat.

"Oh, go on brat. It might do you some good to set foot in a church," Jackie said from the backseat.

"I've had enough of you calling me a brat. I said I'll wait here," he snapped.

This was not working out at all. The last thing I needed was for Rodney and his sister to start arguing with each other. Pastor was expecting us in five minutes.

"Rodney, I want you to come in with me. It won't take long, I promise."

"OK, what is this all about anyway? What's going on Dee-Dee?"

There was no point in keeping the truth from him any longer. He was bound to find out anyway. "I made an appointment for us to meet with Pastor. I really think it will do us some good before we go back to Tennessee."

Rodney's eyes suddenly became slits. "I don't need to go and see no preacher! So this was all a trick to get me over here." He turned around and started yelling at Jackie. "I should have known you had something up your sleeve. Why don't you stay out of my business anyway?"

"Rodney, we need to sit down and talk to someone and I thought it would be a good idea while you were here to…"

"If you want to go in there, then you go, but I'm staying right here." He was adamant and I could think of only one way to get through to him.

"I'm not going to let our baby grow up in a house with parents who are fighting all the time. If that's the way you want it, then I am staying here and raising this baby by myself." I turned to open the door.

He grabbed me by the arm and looked at me in astonishment. "You're pregnant?"

"Yes. It happened when you came home in October. The baby is due in July."

"Why didn't you tell me Dee-Dee?" He relaxed his grip and his eyes softened.

"Because, I don't want to go back to Tennessee and end up having the same problems," I said stubbornly. "This baby can't grow up in an environment like that."

"You need to listen to her…"

"Oh, will you shut up Jackie. This is none of your business anyway," he yelled.

"It is my business. I don't want you to turn out like Daddy. You…"

"How ya'll doing?"

We all turned toward the muffled voice and saw Pastor West standing near the passenger door. He smiled and nodded.

"Good evening," we said in unison.

"Why don't ya'll come on in? It's getting chilly out here."

I looked at Rodney praying that he would come in and meet with the pastor. He hesitated before taking the key out of the ignition and opening the car door.

I sighed deeply. Pastor West held the door for me as I got out of the car.

I rubbed my shoulders and shivered as I walked into the church. Rodney walked in behind me.

Ms. Helen jumped up when she saw all of us walk in. "How you all doing today," she said brightly.

Pastor West turned toward us and looked at me. "Dee-Dee, I want to talk to your husband first and then I want to meet with both of you together. Have a seat over there and I'll call for you."

"Yes, sir," I said nodding and making my way to the chair in the corner.

"And you can have a seat over there as well, young lady," Ms. Helen said, looking at Jackie.

"I'm sorry," I mumbled. "Ms. Helen this is Jackie, my sister-in-law."

Ms. Helen reached out to shake Jackie's hand before ushering us to our seats. Pastor West and Rodney disappeared behind closed doors. It had surprised me that he would want to meet with Rodney alone.

"So how is your mother holding up Dee-Dee? I know she took it pretty hard at the funeral," Ms. Helen said sympathetically.

"She's coming along. It's still hard on her, but she gets a little stronger each day."

"Well that's good to hear and how is school coming along? Your mama must be so proud of you."

"It was fine. The semester ended two weeks ago." I didn't bother to tell her that I would be moving back to Tennessee and would not be returning to school in the spring.

"That's wonderful and did you do well with your grades?"

"I had all A's."

Jackie gave me pat on the back. "That's great!"

"Yes it is," Ms. Helen agreed. She turned back to the letters she had piled on her desk.

Jackie and I waited silently.

I wondered about the conversation going on between the two men in the next room. I glanced at my watch. It had only been fifteen minutes, but it seemed like it was taking forever.

"Do you think he's going to get through to Rodney," I asked Jackie.

She shrugged. "I sure hope so."

We both turned when the door opened and Pastor West motioned for me to come inside. I was nervous as I walked toward him.

"Have a seat next to your husband, Dee-Dee," he said as soon as he closed the door behind me.

I looked over at Rodney. The scowl on his face was cause for concern.

"Your husband and I have been discussing some of the things you shared with me earlier. I wanted to get his take on things since I had talked to you without him having a chance to defend himself," Pastor West said as he moved behind his desk and sat down calmly. He folded his hand across his chest and rocked back and forth in his chair. "Dee-Dee, I do have a question for you. How long have you known that your husband did not want you to work?"

The question caught me completely off guard. "I guess since the beginning," I mumbled.

Pastor West nodded. "So he told you before the two of you got married that he didn't want you to work, but you kept insisting on getting a job," he asked with a penetrating look.

I dropped my head and toyed with the strap on my purse and nodded my head.

Pastor West took a deep breath before continuing. "Now I understand from talking with both of you that the two of you have had several arguments about you working and going to school. Do you think it's fair to be upset with him if he made it clear to you from the beginning that he didn't want his wife to work?"

I shook my head and looked over at Rodney. He smirked and turned away.

"Your husband has also told me that he is not a Christian and that you knew that before the two of you got married."

I nodded my head again.

"Now, the other major cause of concern is of course the spousal abuse."

Rodney stiffened as Pastor West continued. "I have explained to your husband that God did not create women so that their husbands could mistreat them that way. Women are not the property of men to slap around and abuse just because a man is angry. There are better ways to communicate with each other and I would seriously suggest the two of you seek counseling in that area when you get back to Tennessee. It is going to take more than one meeting with me to fix some of the problems that are being addressed here today. Do you understand what I'm saying to you?"

"Yes."

Pastor West held my eyes for a second before turning to look at Rodney. "Would you say that you love your wife?"

Rodney cleared his throat. "Yes sir," he said before looking at me quickly.

"God never intended for you to try to control your wife by abusing her. And I can tell you this, not too many women are going to stay there and continue to take that. They will find a way to get away from all that sooner or later."

Rodney's body stiffened even more as he glared back at Pastor West.

"Dee-Dee, I applaud your efforts to try to get counseling, but you have to know that change has to come from the heart."

This session with Pastor West was not turning out the way I had planned at all. I glanced at Rodney, but he was looking over Pastor West's head at a picture on the wall.

Pastor West continued. "It's going to take some time for the two of you to work through these issues and as I told your husband, I have seen some couples with the same problem come through this and now have a happy marriage. I don't know how it will turn out for the two of you, but my advice to you, Dee-Dee is that it be under the conditions that if this type of abuse happens again, you need to go to the proper authorities. God never intended for marriage to be a death sentence!" Pastor West fixed his eyes on Rodney.

Rodney cleared his throat and I squirmed nervously in my seat as the discussion became increasingly uncomfortable.

"You also need to know that I have talked to Rodney about the fact that he is not a Christian and he says he wants to think about it a little more." Pastor West looked at Rodney again and addressed him in a softer tone. "Please know that I didn't bring you in here to beat up on you." He laughed shortly before continuing, "I know it sure feels like it, but I want to make sure you understand how serious domestic violence is. I want nothing but the best for you two young people and the only way your marriage is going to work is if the two of you can come into agreement on the things I just went over."

I nodded before replying. "Yes sir."

Pastor West looked at both of us before looking over at the clock on the wall. "I'm sorry, but I have another appointment coming in shortly. I'd like to pray with the two of you before you leave. We all bowed our head as Pastor West began by asking God to help us to learn to love and respect each other. Afterward, he stood up and reached his hand over the desk to shake Rodney's hand.

Rodney stood up and shook his hand and waited for me to get up. I thanked Pastor West for meeting with us and followed Rodney out the door. Jackie stood up as soon as we came out of the room. She searched my face for signs of how the meeting had gone. I attempted to smile before waving to Ms. Helen before the three of us headed for the car.

The ride back to the Jackson's house was extremely quiet. We all seemed lost in our own thoughts. I knew that Rodney was still upset and I was debating about the plan to stay the night at his parent's house.

When we pulled into the yard, Ms. Jackson stood up on the porch and looked at us questioningly. "Where did you all run off too?" she asked.

I looked at Jackie not sure how to answer the question.

"Ask them," Rodney said tightly as he walked past her and went into the house.

Mrs. Jackson looked at us frowning. "What's the matter with him?"

"He's mad because Dee-Dee set up a meeting for the two of them to meet with her pastor."

"Without his permission," Mrs. Jackson said with a raised eyebrow.

I realized that none of this worked out the way I had envisioned and I desperately wanted to go home. "I didn't think he would go if he knew," I said softly.

Rodney came back onto the porch and I could tell that he was trying to control his anger.

Mrs. Jackson looked at him and back at us. "Well I'm sure it couldn't have hurt to talk with the pastor, Rodney."

He glared at Jackie before replying, "I don't appreciate you getting into my business."

"Yes, I'm going to get in your business if it means this baby will stay safe," she said defiantly.

"What baby?" Mrs. Jackson repeated.

"Dee-Dee's pregnant," she said as she glared angrily at her brother.

"Well that's wonderful news," Mrs. Jackson said before looking anxiously at Rodney. "Why don't we come in the house and talk about all of this. We don't need the neighbors getting into all our business."

I went into the house reluctantly. Rodney stared at me and refused to turn away.

"Harold, we got some good news. Dee-Dee is pregnant. Rodney is going to be a father."

It was surprising that Mr. Jackson was at home sitting in the kitchen at this time of the day. After looking at him I could see why. One of his legs was in a cast and he was resting it on a pillow. I looked at Jackie hoping that she would explain what had happened.

"He had an accident at work and broke his leg," she whispered.

"And how in the world did that happen if the two of them been apart all this time?"

I stood rooted to the spot unable to believe what I had just heard.

Mrs. Jackson sucked her breath in loudly and clutched her throat.

"She got pregnant the weekend he came home in October, Daddy," Jackie said sarcastically. "The baby is due in July."

Rodney turned his eyes from me and walked over to his father.

"Well you never can tell these days," Mr. Jackson said cuttingly.

"I just want to make sure."

I started moving toward the door. "Why don't you come and sit down Dee-Dee," Mrs. Jackson said quickly.

I looked at Rodney before responding. "I want to go and check on Mama. She's been through a lot lately after Ms. Lucille's death."

"Yes. I was sorry to hear about Lucille's death," Mrs. Jackson said quickly.

Rodney came to stand beside me before I could get out the door. "Why you leaving? You said we were going to stay here tonight."

I refused to look at him because I knew he would see the tears that were threatening to roll down my cheeks.

I pushed the door open and walked onto the porch. "I just want to check on Mama," I said weakly.

"Can't you just give her a call?"

"No," I said angrily and headed toward the steps. He grabbed my arm and pulled me toward him. "Come on Dee-Dee. Enough of these little games for today please."

The tears that I had tried so hard to keep hidden began rushing forth.

"Dee, come on now. What's wrong?"

"So you don't think the baby is yours?" I said through clenched teeth.

"What! Now where in the world did you get that? I never said I didn't believe the baby wasn't mine," he said angrily.

"You didn't answer when your daddy questioned it in there and the expression on your face makes me think that you aren't sure." I was nearing hysteria, but I managed to keep my voice down.

"You're not being fair Dee-Dee. I can't stop what comes out of my father's mouth. If you say the baby is mine, then it's mine."

I roughly brushed the tears away when I heard the door open behind us. "Dee-Dee, don't listen to Daddy. I don't think the man has a heart at all," Jackie said softly.

I nodded and searched my purse for some tissue. Jackie looked in her purse and quickly passed me a napkin. "Sorry, it's all I have."

I wiped away the rest of the tears and thanked her.

Rodney sighed heavily. "Look Dee, I'm sorry Daddy said that. I'm sure he didn't mean it."

"Yeah right," Jackie said.

"Don't you have a house to go to," Rodney yelled at his sister.

"That's exactly where I'm headed Brat!" The two of them glared at each other.

"I need a break too. I want to check on Mama," I said sternly.

"Dee, why are you doing this? I just got home, you set me up to meet with your pastor and now you want to run off because of a stupid comment my daddy made," Rodney whined.

"Dee-Dee, he's right. That was a stupid comment. My father can be heartless at times. Don't let him get to you," Jackie pleaded.

"She's right Dee. You can't let Daddy get to you."

"I need to get out of here," Jackie said. "This has been a long day already. Let me give you a hug in case I don't see you before you leave."

Jackie gave me a quick hug before she turned to leave. "See you later," she said snidely to Rodney over her shoulders.

"Later," he said as he watched her go down the steps.

We watched her back out of the driveway. Jackie beeped her horn before driving off.

"Dee, I know you're upset. I'm upset too, but we need to talk about what happened today. Why didn't you tell me you were planning to go and meet with your pastor?"

"Because you wouldn't have gone with me if I had and you know it," I said defensively.

Rodney sighed. "Probably not, but I didn't like being set up like that. Why do you always want to get other people involved in our business, especially my sister? You told her you were pregnant before you told me," he said accusingly.

"I know I should have told you first, but I just didn't want to go back to the same thing that happened before..."

"Why do you keep bringing that up?" he said angrily. "Look, I agree that we went through a lot, but we had some good times too."

I pulled away from him and sat down on the step. He sat down beside me. "Rodney, how are you going to learn how to control your temper if we don't get some help?"

Pastor West talked to me about that today and he gave me some suggestions, but Dee, you do some things to cause me to go off too."

"You can't keep blaming me when you lose your temper."

"I'm not blaming you, but how are we going to work through our problems if you keep bringing up the past and nagging me about working and going to school?"

"I'm not trying to nag you, but we can't work through anything if you keep going off every time we have an argument. We need some help."

"OK, we'll find somebody when we get to Tennessee, if that's what you want," he said reluctantly.

I looked at Rodney to see if he was being serious. I wanted to believe him and prayed silently that this was the sign that I was looking for.

❧ *Chapter 16* ❧

The day had come for us to leave. It was hard to pull myself together and to keep from falling apart. I didn't want to make things even worse for Mama. Rodney wasted no time getting my things loaded in the car. Saying goodbye to Mama was just as hard as it was the first time when I moved to Tennessee. It didn't seem right to leave her alone so soon after the death of one of her dearest friends.

Rodney was very careful around Mama and tried not to say much. He avoided being alone with her as much as possible. He also didn't say anything to me about my car sitting in Ms. Pearls' yard. I guess he was just glad that I was going to Tennessee with him and he didn't want to get into an argument about it.

Ms. Pearl came over right before we left. She gave me a big hug and told me not to worry about the car because she was going to take good care of it. "You take care of yosef now Dee-Dee and don't fret none bout Hattie. I'll keep an eye on her."

"I know you will. I'll call as soon as I can." She squeezed my hand before whispering to me softly, "Don't let that boy hit on you no more. You put him in jail if you have to, but don't let him put his hand on you again."

I nodded before giving her another quick hug. I hugged Mama tightly before joining Rodney in the car. We both waved before pulling out of the driveway. I tried to stop the tears from falling, but it was impossible. We were on the Interstate before I finally stopped crying.

Rodney broke the silence and started talking about the baby. "I can't believe we're having a baby…" he kept repeating over and over again. He was silent for a minute. "When did you find out?" He glanced at me with a raised eyebrow.

"I've known for sure for a couple of weeks. I didn't want to believe it at first and I wanted to tell you face to face this time."

We were both silent after that statement. I'm sure it made him think about what happened the last time when I had written to him about my pregnancy. He had insisted that he never got the letter. I wanted to kick myself. Why did I have to bring that up now and spoil the moment?

"Do you want a boy or girl?" I had to say something to change the subject.

Rodney shrugged and then looked at me and laughed. "I hope it's a boy. I would rather have a son first so that he can take care of his baby sister later." He winked and laughed.

We remained silent for a long time after that, lost in our thoughts. I tried to convince myself that I was happy, but deep inside, I was fearful of what the future held for us. *Would things turn out the way they did the last time?* Rodney said that we would go to see a counselor, and I desperately wanted to believe him.

"What will we name her if she's a girl?"

"I'm sure we'll come up with something, but it's going to be a boy. I just know it."

"Just in case it's not, we need to think of a name for a girl." We began calling out names to each other, laughing at the old fashioned ones. We talked about the baby until we stopped for lunch. Surprisingly, I was able to eat most of what I ordered at Burger King.

When we got back on the road, it didn't take long for me to fall asleep. I was disappointed when I woke up hours later to find out that I had missed seeing the mountains that had mesmerized me the first time we traveled this way.

"We only have about four hours left to go. Where do you want to stop for dinner?"

I shrugged. "I don't care. I'm still full from lunch."

"I'll just wait and look for a place when we get closer to Nashville."

"That's fine."

After a quick trip to the restroom, we were on the road again. I tried desperately to stay awake to keep him company, but it wasn't long before I felt myself drifting off again. We stopped at Wendy's in Nashville, but I still wasn't hungry, so I ordered some fries and a Coke. Rodney ordered two sandwiches and ate like he hadn't eaten all day. It still amazed me how he managed to stay so skinny the way he ate.

"Do you want me to drive," I asked when we got back in the car.

"I got it. We're almost there now."

It was the answer I expected, but I thought I'd ask anyway. I tried to picture what the new apartment would look like. There was no way it could be worse than the last one we had. It wasn't long before I had fallen asleep again.

"We're here Dee."

Rodney's voice startled me. It took a few minutes to figure out where we were. We were parked in front of an apartment in Lee Village. I drove by these apartments often when Rodney was away for military training and dreamed about the day that we would be able to move into one of them. At the time, they looked so much better than the ratty apartment we had off post.

Rodney waited for me to get out of the car. He was smiling broadly as we walked toward the building. It was dark when we arrived, so it was hard to get a good look at our surroundings. Rodney opened the door quickly and stepped aside for me to go in.

The rooms were much bigger and this time we had matching furniture. "This is nice."

Rodney nodded and closed the door behind us. "They delivered the furniture on Friday. Not bad huh? You look around. I'll get the things out of the car."

I headed straight for the bedroom. There was full size bed with a walnut headboard sitting in the middle of the room between the double windows. There were two nightstands on either side of the bed and a large dresser with a mirror. This was most certainly a step up for us. There was a bathroom in our bedroom and there was a half bath down the hall. Yes, this was definitely, a lot better.

When I walked into the kitchen, I opened every cabinet. Rodney walked in with the last bag and stood in the middle of the living room.

"Do you like it?"

I smiled and nodded. "Yes, this is a mansion compared to our last apartment." I looked at him quickly hoping that I hadn't hurt his feeling about the last apartment. He nodded in agreement.

"Yeah, that last one was a dump."

I felt relieved that he thought so too. "You hungry?"

"No. I'm good, but we need to go to the Commissary in the morning. I didn't have a chance to buy groceries."

I walked over to the refrigerator and looked in. He was right. The only thing in there was a gallon of milk and some sliced cheese.

"There's some cereal in the cabinet. We can have that for breakfast."

I nodded and looked at my watch. "I need to call Mama and let her know that we had a safe trip."

"We have a phone in our bedroom, one in the kitchen and one in here," Rodney said pointing to the phone on the end table by the loveseat.

I quickly dialed the numbers and waited anxiously for Mama to answer.

"Hello."

"Hey Mama, we got here alright."

"Hey Baby. I'm glad to hear that ya'll made it. Were you OK during the trip?"

I knew that she worried about me getting sick on the road. "I did fine. I only got sick to my stomach once, but it passed quickly." I pulled my legs up under me and got comfortable on the sofa. I could see Rodney out of the corner of my eyes as he walked into the bedroom and lay across the bed.

"How you doing Mama?"

"Today was better. Everyday gets a little easier. Pearl came by for a bit and we went to the store to pick up a few packages."

I was happy to hear that they were already beginning to put the car to use. "That's good Mama. Was Ms. Pearl all excited about driving it?"

"You know she was. That woman smiled most of the way there and back. That was nice of you to leave the car Dee-Dee."

"I'm just glad that you and Ms. Pearl will make good use of it, that's all."

We talked for another few minutes before hanging up. I looked in on Rodney in the bedroom. He was fast asleep.

I went back to the living room and started unpacking some of our bags. I looked through the kitchen cabinet and wondered what Rodney had done with the things we had purchased for the last apartment. A few minutes later, I sat down and took in the room around me. Hopefully, we would be happier here. *God, I hope I didn't make a mistake in trusting this man again.*

❧ *Chapter 17* ❧

I had been back for a little over two months now and we were beginning to settle in nicely. I still had my moments of suspicions, but it was never any thing that I could put my finger on. There were a few times when he lost his temper, but he usually just stormed out of the house. He seemed to be doing everything he could not to lay a hand on me. I was sure it was because of what happened the last time when he caused me to lose the baby.

I was almost five months along and we were looking forward to the birth of the baby. We hadn't managed to settle on a name, because Rodney refused to consider names for girls. He insisted that there was no point in thinking about names for girls because he was certain that I was having a boy.

"What if it's a girl? We need to pick out a name just in case," I argued.

"It's a boy, so we don't need to think of a name for a girl."

"What will we do if it's a girl? We are going to have to try to come up with a name in the hospital in a hurry," I whined.

"Well, you can think of names of girls if you want, but it's going to be a boy. I just know it."

It was pointless to try to argue with him. He had his mind made up and there was no talking him out of it.

My belly was beginning to swell and now it was easier to tell that I was pregnant. One day after trying to get Rodney to at least tell me what he thought of the name that I came up with if the baby happened to be a girl, he kneeled in front of me and rubbed my swollen belly. "Hey son, I keep trying to tell your mama that there's a little boy in there, but she won't listen to me."

I laughed and shook my head. "You are silly."

He had the silliest grin on his face as he continued to pat my stomach. Looking down at him made me remember the man I married almost two years ago. As I thought about that day, it was hard to believe all that we had been through.

"I gotta go. We got formation at one o'clock and I can't be late."
I watched him as he grabbed his cap and walked to the door.

"We might be working late to get things ready for this field problem. I'll see you later," he said and he was gone.

I stood there for a few minutes before cleaning up the dishes we had used for lunch. It was hard to take Rodney at his word and simply believe him when he said he would be working late. I kept thinking about the times he lied to me before about working late when he was actually spending time with another woman. We hadn't had any major confrontations that would prove whether or not he had truly changed. I was hopeful that things would continue to get better for us. It was not going to be easy to forget the past and all that had happened, but I was hoping for the best.

The sharp shrill of the phone behind me made me jump. It rang a second time before I picked it up.

"Hello."

"Hey Baby."

"Hey Mama, how you doing?"

"I'm comin' along. I just called to check on you and see how ya'll was doin'. Everything OK wid the baby?"

"Everything is fine. I had an appointment last week and the doctor said that everything looks good. He thinks that I will have the baby on July 26."

"That's good Baby. How Rodney?"

I knew what Mama really meant and I wanted to erase all of her fears so that she wouldn't worry about me. "Rodney is doing fine and we are doing much better. He really seems to be trying Mama."

"That's good to hear. I just wanted to check on you and make sure everything goin' alright."

"How are you and Ms. Pearl doing?" I knew that the two of them were still mourning the death of Ms. Lucille.

"We doing fine. It's still hard to believe that Lucille gone though. I miss her."

Mama was silent.

"I'm glad you called Mama. I miss you a lot and I'm sorry I can't be there right now for you and Ms. Pearl."

"Oh, don't worry 'bout me none. We gonna be just fine. It takes time to get over losing people you care about."

"I know, but Ms. Lucille's death made me miss Daddy more than ever," I blurted out before thinking about how my words would affect Mama. I put my hand over my mouth quickly and immediately regretted my words. "I'm sorry Mama. I didn't mean to bring up Daddy."

"Chile, I don't mind if you talk 'bout your daddy. He was your father and it's only natural that you would miss him. That ain't gonna change."

"I know, but I don't want you to be sad. It took you so long to get over his death."

"Baby, people say that you supposed to forget as time pass. That ain't true Dee-Dee. When you lose people you love, you just learn how to deal with the pain a little better the more time go by."

"I thought it always made you sad when somebody mentioned Daddy."

Mama chuckled. "Is that why you never talk about your daddy? It's good for you to talk about him and remember him. He was a good man and I know you miss him as much as I do. Yes, sometimes you see me cry, but it's not because I'm in a lot of pain. He was my husband and my best friend. I enjoyed being wid him. There ain't nobody who could make me laugh like that man. We enjoyed doing things together and that's what I miss the most."

Mama and I talked for another fifteen minutes. She updated me on everything that was going on in the neighborhood and at the church.

"Baby, I gotta go now. I just wanted to check on ya'll. Take care and let me know if you need anything."

"I love you Mama. Bye."

It always made me feel good to talk to Mama. I never realized just how special my parents' relationship had been. I could only hope that one day Rodney and I would have the same type of relationship. She had sounded really good on the phone, and that took some of the worry away. She worried about me and I worried about her. "Lord, please keep Mama safe," I prayed softly before clearing the leftovers away.

It wasn't long before I was busy with chores and planning the meal for dinner. At least I had more time since Rodney would be working late. After cleaning up and putting things away, I sat down at the table and looked through my list of baby names. Rodney may not want to discuss the possibility that we could have a girl, so coming up with a name would be left to me. I wanted to be ready if things didn't turn out as he had planned.

After reviewing my list and adding a few more names, I said each of them out loud to see if I could find one that was just right. I kept revising the list of names until I got sleepy and decided to take a quick nap.

I jumped up and stared at the clock. It was almost five o'clock! My nap had lasted longer than I had planned. Thankfully, Rodney was working late. It didn't take as long as I thought to fix dinner. I glanced at the clock again and wondered what time Rodney would be getting home.

I decided to give Francine a call. I had only seen her once since I came back to Tennessee. Things were a bit awkward for us at first; partly because I felt ashamed to be back here with Rodney after all he had put me through. But it didn't take long for us to move past that and rekindle our friendship.

Francine answered the phone on the first ring.

"Hello," she said sounding like she was out of breath.

"Hey, it's me. I just wanted to call and say hello."

"Claudette. It's good to hear from you. You were on my mind. How are things going with you?"

"Things are good. You sound like you've been running or something."

Francine laughed. "I need to get my big behind out there and go running." She laughed again. "I just got in. I had to make two trips outside to bring my groceries in. So what's going on?"

"Nothing much. I was waiting for my husband to get home. I thought he would be here by now." I immediately regretted telling her that. I didn't want her to think that Rodney was up to his old tricks again.

Instead of responding to my comment, Francine changed the subject. "So how's the pregnancy coming along? Is everything OK with the baby?"

"Things are good. The last time I went, the doctor said that everything looked good. I'm still not showing that much though."

"That could be a good thing. You won't have to spend a lot of money on maternity clothes."

I laughed. "Yeah, that is a good thing." I heard a key in the door and turned to see Rodney come in with a nasty scowl on his face. He nodded to me before taking off his cap and plopping down into the loveseat. It was obvious that he had not had a good day.

"I gotta go. Rodney just got home. I'll talk to you later."

"Not a problem. Bye."

I hung up the phone and looked at Rodney. His demeanor had not changed.

"So who was that?"

"Francine," I said nonchalantly.

"Oh, Heavy Mama," he said sarcastically.

I frowned and got up from the sofa. "You ready to eat?"

"No. I just want to sit here for a minute. I'll eat later."

His answer surprised me. I stopped and turned to look at him again. "Is something wrong?"

"Naw, I just need to rest a bit. We've been moving boxes and furniture all day. I'm tired."

I walked back toward the sofa and sat down. "Alright."

"So what's Wide Load talking about these days?"

It was hard to talk to Rodney when he got in one of his moods, so I did my best to ignore his barbs. "I know you don't like Francine, but she's a nice person."

"No, I don't like her. She tried to break us up, her and Preacher Boy. You been talkin' to him too?"

"Look, I don't know what you're all worked up about, but you…"

"You didn't answer my question. You been talkin' to him too?"

I could feel myself beginning to get angry. "No. I have not talked to Walter." I held his stare.

"You can say what you want, but I know Preacher Boy wanted you. I'm sure it broke his heart when he found out we were back together."

"Just like Teresa Collins wanted you right?" I snapped.

Rodney's face became rigid and his eyes narrowed.

I got up and walked toward the bedroom. "Let me know when you're ready to eat." I closed the bedroom door behind me.

I turned on the little TV that we had moved into the bedroom after we bought the new one for Rodney. I lay across the bed and tried to calm myself down. A few minutes later Rodney came in the room and plopped down on the bed beside me. It was hard to miss the strong smell of alcohol on his breath.

"I guess you mad now, huh?"

I didn't bother to answer.

"You not talkin' to me now?" He clutched my face and turned it toward him and smiled. "It's just me and you now Baby. Oh, I forgot and Junior," he said as he let go of my face and patted my stomach.

Rodney rolled over to his side to look at the TV and few minutes later, he was snoring loudly.

I got up and went back into the living room. He had left his shirt and boots in the middle of the floor. I stepped over them and went into the kitchen to put the food away. I fumed as I thought about the way he had come home reeking of liquor. Today was Thursday; Happy Hour at the Enlisted club. Apparently, he and his buddies had decided to go out and get drunk after work. *He'll be out like a light until tomorrow morning.*

After putting the food away and cleaning the kitchen, I sat down on the sofa and looked for a good movie to watch. My mind drifted as I flipped through the channels. Finally, I gave up and turned the TV off. I thought about how passionate I had been about us going for counseling before coming back up here. I hadn't once tried to find a counselor and I was beginning to see some of Rodney's old habits creeping in again. This was unsettling for me. Why hadn't I sought the help of marriage counselor? After his stunt tonight, it was obvious that we still needed to seek professional help.

❧ Chapter 18 ❦

I was up early the next morning. Today was one of the days Rodney had PT. I was still having a hard time getting up at five o'clock in the morning, because it was hard to go back to sleep. He said he enjoyed the physical training because it helped to keep him in shape. He often bragged about how he was one of the few soldiers who didn't fall out of formation when they had to do the five mile run with the unit commander. Thankfully, he only had to do it three days a week.

As soon as the door closed behind him, I got up and started looking in the phone book for a marriage counselor. I found four names and jotted them down. It was still early, so I decided to wait awhile before I started calling around. *Would Rodney still be willing to go with me?* That was the big question and I wasn't sure how to answer it. He had promised to go, but that could have been his ploy to get me to agree to move back up here. *What if he refused to go?*

I decided to get my housework done and wash a load of clothes before calling. After working steadily, I decided to take a quick break. I glanced at the clock and picked up the phone to make my first call. I talked to the receptionists and tried to get as much information as I could before making my decision. They all wanted to know if I had insurance. By the time I got off the phone, I was more than a little discouraged. I knew that Rodney would refuse to pay anything, even if it was only twenty dollars to get marriage counseling.

What do I do now? I shook my head as I tried to think of another plan. Suddenly I felt a twitch in my stomach. I sat up and put my hand on my belly in time to feel a flutter of movement that felt like butterflies moving around inside of me. I smiled as I realized what was happening. I had just felt my baby move for the first time. I held my hand there for a few minutes until the movements stopped.

I reached for the phone and called Mama. I couldn't stop myself from smiling and I needed to tell somebody about what I had just experienced. Mama answered on the third ring.

"Hello," she said sounding out of breath.

"Mama, it's me. I just felt the baby move," I exclaimed excitedly.

Mama started to laugh. "That's wonderful Baby. Soon that baby gonna be movin' so much, she gonna keep you up at night."

"I'm looking forward to that."

"Humph, you say that now, but you won't be sayin' that when the time come. I can remember you rolling around so much inside me, I thought sure you was gonna be a ballerina or somethin' like that. Most nights I could barely get any sleep."

I laughed. "They move around that much?" The idea of being able to feel my baby moving around inside of me was wonderful and miraculous.

"You just wait. Sometimes those babies start pokin' around and you'll be able to feel the little arms and legs when you touch your stomach."

Mama and I talked on and on about the baby. I didn't realize how long we had been talking until I heard my stomach growl and looked up at the clock. I was shocked to discover that we had been on the phone for almost an hour.

"Mama, I gotta get off this phone. We've been talking for almost an hour."

"Lawd, I guess we got all caught up in talkin' about babies. I'll send some money to help you pay the bill."

"You don't have to do that Mama. We'll pay it," I said as I thought about how I was going to do that without Rodney finding out.

"No, I'll send some money for the bill."

I knew that there was no point in arguing. She was going to send it anyway.

"I love you Mama, bye."

I hung up and stared at the clock. Rodney was planning to come home for lunch and it was almost lunch time. I got up and quickly fixed a couple sandwiches from the pork chops we had last night. As soon as I finished, I felt the cold air on my back and knew that I had finished just in time.

"Hey, I don't have long. I gotta get some paperwork ready before our formation." He plopped down on the sofa and threw his cap on the coffee table. I added some chips to the plate and grabbed a Coke out of the refrigerator. I put the plate on the tray and walked into the living room. "Guess what?"

He looked up at me and waited for me to go on. "I felt the baby move today," I said excitedly.

Rodney smiled and reached for the tray. "What did it feel like?"

"It almost felt like butterflies flying around in there."

Rodney put his hand on my stomach and kept it there for a few seconds. "I guess he wore himself out and went to sleep, because I don't feel anything," he said before turning his attention back to the lunch in front of him.

I went back into the kitchen to fix myself a sandwich. When I returned to the living room, I froze when I saw Rodney looking at the note I left on the table about the marriage counselors. The phone book was lying beside him.

He took a deep breath and looked up at me as I stood there with the tray in my hand. "Why you keep trying to make it seem like we got problems with our marriage Dee-Dee? I think we're doing better than a lot of couples, but it seems like you looking for problems," he said as he came back in the living room and stood over me.

His eyes held mine. "I already told you. We don't need to be tellin' people our business. Those people are nothin' but quacks anyway."

I swallowed the food in my mouth quickly. "It's not a shrink, Rodney. They can help us learn to communicate with each other," I said.

"Communicate with each other? That's exactly what we're doing right now. Why do we need somebody to tell us how to talk to each other? That's just a waste of money. There is nothing wrong with our marriage and I wish you would stop trying to make it seem like it is."

This was going to be an uphill battle. I didn't see how I was ever going to get him to go to counseling with me.

Rodney grabbed his cap from the table and pulled it down on his head forcefully. "I'll be home late. We need to get some things cleared out of the warehouse and it could take awhile."

Somehow I was not surprised by his last statement. He had been working late more often lately and I was beginning to be suspicious.

"Later," he said as he walked toward the door. He turned to look at me before walking out the door. I kept my eyes glued to the TV as if I hadn't heard him.

As soon as the door closed behind him, I got up and took the tray into the kitchen, throwing away the half-eaten sandwich. I pounded my fist on the counter in frustration. *God, I can't believe I fell for this again.* I was angry at Rodney, but angrier with myself. I pulled out a chair and sat down at the table.

Why didn't I insist on the counseling before coming back to him? What I hoped would change in the relationship was not any better than when I was here before.

I got up and went to look out of the window. The sun was shining brightly on this March morning. *A walk might do me some good.* I got my coat and gloves from the closet and grabbed my key out of my purse. As soon as I stepped outside the door, the chilly air sliced through me. The sunlight had been deceiving.

I decided to brave the cold and walk around the neighborhood anyway. There were only a few cars in the driveway and the streets were virtually empty. The children were still in school and the soldiers wouldn't be home for hours.

"Cold out here today, isn't it?"

I turned in the direction of the voice to see a young woman with wavy blonde hair walking toward me.

I slowed down to answer her question. "Yes, it is. I didn't think it would be cold out here when I looked out of the window and saw the sun shining so brightly."

She started walking beside me and looked up at the sky. "I know. I was thinking the same thing. That's why I decided to come out too. Mind if I join you?"

"No, I don't mind, but I don't know how long I'm going to be out here. It's getting too cold for me."

"No problem. I probably won't be out here long either. So what's your name? I'm Kristen. Most people just call me Kristy."

I smiled again before responding. "My name is Claudette."

"I'm pleased to meet you, Claudette. So how long have you been living on post? I haven't seen you before.

"We moved in right after Christmas."

"Oh, so where were you stationed before?"

"We've only been here."

"It won't be long before your husband will be getting orders then. This is our third duty station. Well, I should say his third and my second. We were stationed at Fort Knox. Then they sent him to Korea for a year and now we're here."

"So where did you live when your husband went to Korea?"

"I could have stayed on the base at Knox, but I decided to move back home with my parents until he came back," Kristen said lightly.

We walked for about twenty minutes before my ears started stinging and my nose began to run. Thankfully, I had put a wad of tissue in my pocket on Saturday when Rodney and I had gone to the Commissary to shop for groceries. My body shivered uncontrollably.

"Are you ready to turn around?" Kristen asked when she saw me shivering.

"Yeah, I think I've had enough, how about you?"

"Yea, it's way too cold for me today. Do you want to stop in for some hot chocolate to warm up a bit? My house isn't that far away."

"That sounds good."

When we reached her apartment I rubbed my arms up and down briskly and waited for her to open the door. Kristen stepped aside to let me in first. I walked in and took off my coat. Kristen reached for it and gave me a look of surprise.

"You have a little one on the way. Is it your first?"

I nodded.

"Well congratulations! When are you due?"

"In July," I replied.

She ushered me into the kitchen. Their apartment looked exactly like ours, but it wasn't furnished with government furniture. "Nice furniture," I commented as I followed her to the table.

"Thanks. We bought a lot of this stuff when we were at Knox. It didn't take long for me to get tired of the government issued stuff."

We both laughed. I sat down at the table and watched her get the kettle ready for the hot chocolate. "So do you have kids?"

"Yes, we have twin girls, Bria and Bryann. They should be home in about an hour."

"Wow, was it hard having two babies at the same time?"

"Yes it was," Kristen exclaimed loudly. "But my husband, Brian, was wonderful. He was right there with me and things just worked themselves out. That was another reason that I decided to move back in with my parents when he went to Korea. My parents simply adore the girls and they always complain that they want to be able to see them more."

"I know. That's going to be tough for me too. My mom lives in South Carolina, so she's not going to be able to see the baby often."

We chatted back and forth until the front door flew open and two beautiful little girls, with a head full of curly blonde hair came rushing in. "We're home," they cried in unison.

Kristen put her cup down and stood up. She opened her arms and the girls raced toward her. "How was your day?" Kristen hugged them both and brushed their hair away from their little faces.

"Fine," they said before turning toward me.

One of them moved shyly toward me and smiled. "What's your name?"

"Girls say hello to Claudette," Kristen piped in. "She lives a few houses down. We were just enjoying a cup of hot chocolate."

"We want some hot chocolate," they said as they jumped up and down.

I got up and walked toward the living room. "I should be going."

"You don't have to run off," Kristen said looking at me pleadingly.

"No, I really need to go. I need to get dinner ready."

"OK, but don't be a stranger. Maybe we can go walking again some time, she said as she walked toward me. Let me get your number and I'll give you a call sometime."

"Sure," I said waiting for her to get something to write with.

Bria walked over to me and pointed to my stomach. "You gotta baby in there."

I nodded. "Yes."

"Can I touch it?"

"Bria honey, that's not nice to go around asking people to touch their bellies," Kristen scolded when she came back into the living room.

"It's alright," I said looking down at Bria. She put her hand on my stomach and quickly snatched it away before putting her hands over her mouth to cover her giggles.

Bryann walked over to me. "I want to feel the baby too," she whined.

Kristen looked at me and shook her head apologetically. Before I could respond, she patted my belly lightly and started giggling along with her sister.

"Girls, go and change your school clothes, while I say goodbye to Claudette. When you're done, I'll fix you some hot chocolate."

"Yeah," the girls cheered loudly as they ran upstairs.

"I'm sorry Claudette."

"It's no problem Kristen. It's OK."

"Put your number here." She pushed a tablet toward me and turned to reach for my jacket in the closet.

I scribbled my number quickly and reached for my coat. "Thanks for the hot chocolate. I enjoyed our conversation."

"So did I. I'll give you a call to see when you want to go walking again."

I waved before walking out the door. "See ya."

It was still very chilly outside, so I made my way home quickly.

❧ *Chapter 19* ❧

As my pregnancy progressed over the next few months, I began to ache more and more. My stomach seemed to be stretched as far as it could possibly go and I still had a month and a half to go. My doctor kept insisting that I could still stand to gain a few more pounds. I found that hard to believe because I was eating everything in sight. I was having a difficult time resting at night, partly because I favored sleeping on my stomach and that was no longer an option. I looked for every available opportunity to nap during the day to make up for the sleep that I was losing at night.

Mama called to check on me regularly. I was also spending a lot of time with Kristen. I enjoyed talking to her and learning about her family. I thought about her as I cleaned the house. She seemed to have the perfect family. She had two adorable little girls and a husband who was still madly in love with her. One day as she talked about her family, she told me that her parents were upset when she got married in her first year of college.

Kristen sighed. "I have to admit that I did intend to finish school before we started a family, but a year after we were married the girls were born, and it has been hard trying to get back in school. I did take some classes when Brian went to Korea, but I didn't stick with it."

"How do your parents feel about your marriage now," I asked.

"They love Brian. It took awhile for that to happen though. My dad thought that we were too young to start a family, and they weren't thrilled about the amount of time that Brian was away. I must say that over the years, my dad has told me that Brian is a good man and he has earned his respect."

"That's wonderful. My mom didn't want me to marry Rodney," I confessed. "She told me that if I married him, I would be unequally yoked because he wasn't a Christian." I looked at Kristen to see her reaction.

She nodded before responding. "I can understand why she felt that way. My parents probably would have refused to come to the wedding if Brian hadn't been a Christian. That was one of the first questions my father asked him when he came over to meet them."

"Do you really think it makes that much of a difference?"

Kristen nodded. "I do Claudette. It just seems like there could be a lot of division over key issues and being married is already hard enough. That's not to say that you can't be unequally yoked with someone who says that they are a Christian. I know a lot of couples who later got divorced and they were both raised in the church."

I was confused. "So how do you know for sure if he's the right one?"

Kristen sighed before answering. "It really has more to do with what's in a person's heart. There are a lot of people who call themselves Christians, but they don't have a relationship with the Lord."

Kristen laughed when she saw my expression. "Let me explain what I mean. Someone who is in relationship with the Lord understands how much He loves them and they know that He expects them to love others the same way. The love of God is reflected in the way we treat others."

"You're talking about the Golden Rule."

Kristen smiled. "Well, yes that's what it boils down to. When we do right by others, we honor the one who created them."

I thought about what she said. "So before you marry someone, you should look to see how they treat other people?"

"Certainly, but that takes time. You have to get to know someone before you just jump into marriage. Brian and I went together for years before we got married. I knew his family and his friends. We got to be friends first."

"The two of you seem to have a great marriage," I said.

Kristen laughed. "Don't get me wrong, we have our moments and disagreements just like everyone else, but I know that he loves me and the girls and he wouldn't do anything to hurt us. But I can tell you that a lot of that is the result of his relationship with the Lord. So how did you meet your husband?"

Her question caught me off guard. I frowned and thought about where to start. I told her that Rodney and I met in high school and about how he had swept me off my feet.

"I agree that your husband is a very handsome man. I thought that the very first time I met him, but the two of you seem so different."

"What do you mean?" I asked steeling myself for her answer.

"Don't get me wrong, I think the two of you make a cute couple, but you seem so easy going and sincere. Your husband's demeanor is just the opposite."

I thought about her comments for a long time when I got home that day and wished that we had taken the time to get to know each other. Pastor West was right. I couldn't blame Rodney for being upset about me working if I knew that's what he said from the start. I had cheated myself when I decided to throw away my dream of going to college and becoming a nurse.

After cleaning the house, I found a comfortable spot on the sofa and tried to relax. I nodded off briefly before the piercing sound of the phone rang out beside me. I jumped and tried to gather myself. I reached for the phone and answered on the second ring.

"Hello,"

"Hey. It's me, Francine."

"How are you," I said pulling myself up slowly.

"Good. I just wanted to see how you were doing. I just got back in town from my vacation."

"So how was it?"

"Girl, I had so much fun. I wanted to stay for a few more days."

I'm glad you had a good time. Maybe Rodney and I will go one day. I've never been to Myrtle Beach."

"And you're from South Carolina. Girl, what are you waiting on?"

"That's a good question," I said laughing.

"So how are things going with you?"

I knew that Francine was talking about Rodney and me. "Things are about the same. Rodney tries to call at least once a day. I guess he wants to make sure he's there if something happens with the baby."

"Well that's a good thing. Maybe he's coming around and getting his priorities straight. He hasn't tried to get physical with you has he?"

"No, I don't think he wants to take a chance on having anything bad happen to the baby. He remembers that we lost the last baby because of his temper."

"That's good to hear. Let's hope he keeps feeling the same way after the baby is born."

Rodney had come very close a few times and I was thankful that I was pregnant or things could have turned out differently. We always seemed to argue after he had been out drinking with his buddies. "So what are you doing this weekend?"

Francine sighed. "I'm relaxing and getting myself ready to go back to work. I think I need a vacation after the vacation."

We both laughed.

"Oh, and I meant to tell you that I stuck to my diet. I didn't over do it."

"That's good. I knew you could do it."

"Yeah, I was surprised too. Girl, you know I wanted that funnel cake and ice cream. My mouth watered every time somebody walked by me eating some."

I chuckled and shook my head. "That's funny. My doctor is trying to get me to gain weight."

"I wish I could send about fifty pounds your way."

"I don't think I want that much. He says I only need to gain about ten."

"Man, life is just not fair. Your doctor wants you to gain weight and here I am trying to lose some."

"So how much have you lost?"

"Let's just say I didn't lose anymore, but I didn't gain any either."

"I bet that was hard being on vacation and all."

"You know it, girl, but I need to keep losing. I went walking every day to make up for all the extras I had eaten."

"I hope I'll be able to recognize you the next time I see you."

We both laughed.

There was no telling when we would be able to get together again. We normally tried to have lunch together when Rodney left for training. He didn't like Francine. He blamed her and Walter for trying to break up our marriage.

We had a good laugh as we continued to talk about her vacation. "Look, I need to get off this phone, but before I go, make sure you call and let me know when you have the baby. That will probably be the only time I get to see you is while you're in the hospital."

I knew that she was right. Francine knew how Rodney felt about her and even though she would never come out and say it, I knew that she felt the same way about him.

"First chance I get, I will give you a call."

"Don't forget now, because I may not be working on the day

you come in."

"I promise."

"OK. I gotta go."

"Bye."

I smiled and shook my head when I hung up the phone. I enjoyed talking to Francine and wished we could get together more often. She rarely talked about Walter and when she did, it was only to highlight something about her church. She never failed to mention that I should try to find a church home somewhere. She knew things would be extremely awkward if I were to start coming to her church.

She wasn't the only one getting on my case about finding a church. Mama mentioned it almost every time I talked to her. I wished I could go to Francine's church though. I had enjoyed the sermons and the choir was pretty good too.

Looking for a church home was something that I needed to work on. I wanted my baby to be christened and raised in the church as I had been. But I knew that Rodney wouldn't want to go with me and he would probably find some excuse not to go.

Kristen had invited me to come to her church and that was another option that I was considering. Brian and Kristen regularly talked about their faith and how important it was in helping them grow together as a family. I was very impressed with their home life and wished that mine could be the same. When I visited her home, it reminded me of the environment in which I had grown up.

I rested my hand on my protruding belly. The baby was moving around. I smiled. What had began as flutters a few months ago now felt like somersaults. I smiled. *You are going to be very active aren't you?* If the baby was a boy, he would certainly take after Rodney in that area. I tended to be more subdued.

I got up to check the mail when I heard the mail truck outside. As soon as I stepped outside, I heard the phone ring behind me. I decided to ignore it and get the mail instead. I could hear the phone ringing again as I waddled back inside trying to move as fast as I could, but it was too late. *Whoever it is will call back.*

I flipped through the letters and smiled when I saw the letter from Mama. I quickly dropped the other letters on the counter and opened hers. She had sent me some money to cover the last phone call and some money to buy a toy for the baby. What would I ever do without Mama? I fixed myself a nice tall glass of iced tea and settled in at the table to answer her letter. When I finished, Rodney burst through the door. I looked up in astonishment.

He looked stunned to find me sitting at the table. That expression soon turned into an scowl. "Why didn't you answer the phone?" He slammed the door and walked over to me trying to catch his breath.

"I went out to get the mail. When I came back the phone had stopped ringing," I said defensively.

"I called twice. I raced home thinking something had happened," he snapped. He threw his cap on the table and wiped the sweat from his forehead.

"I'm sorry, but I tried to get to the phone in time."

Rodney shook his head and stomped over to the refrigerator. He grabbed a Coke and downed it in a matter of seconds. He walked to the counter and scanned the mail.

"I might as well stay and have lunch. It's almost lunchtime anyway." He went back to the refrigerator and pulled the door open gruffly. He kept the angry scowl on his face as he looked inside. He pulled out the leftover meatloaf and walked over to the counter. I watched him as he made himself a sandwich. What surprised me is that he didn't wait for me to fix it for him.

Rodney put his plate on a tray and looked over at me. "What mail came?"

I shoved the letters toward him. "Just a few bills and a letter from Mama, I said before realizing that the money was still lying on the table." Too late! We both looked at the money at the same time.

"I guess your mama still don't think I can take care of you," he said sarcastically before biting into his sandwich.

"No, she just wanted to send some money to pay for the phone bill. We talked for a long time and she said she would send some money to pay it," I said hurriedly.

Rodney put his sandwich down and gave me a hard glare. "We've been through this already Dee-Dee. Why you gotta stay on the phone with your mom for hours?" He walked toward me and snatched the letters from the table before going into the living room.

I started to reply to his last question, but decided against it. *Might as well let him calm down*, I thought. He turned on the TV and began watching The Price is Right. It was interesting to me that I could be home all day without turning on the television, but that was the first thing he did when he walked through the door. It almost seemed like he hated to give himself time to think.

I folded the letter to Mama and went to look for an envelope in the bedroom. I heard the doorbell and wondered who would be paying us a visit this time of the day. I heard Rodney get up and go to the door.

When I came out of the room, I smiled when I saw Kristen standing there.

"Hey, I made a key lime pie and thought you might like a piece," she said as she shoved a small dish in my direction.

"Thanks, I said taking it from her. Let me put it in something so you can take the dish back with you."

Rodney sat down and continued eating as if we weren't there. He had met Kristen before and so far, he didn't have any objections to our friendship.

Kristen followed me into the kitchen. "So what are your plans for the day? "

I shrugged. "I'll probably stay in and go for a walk later this afternoon. It's hot out there."

"Yes it is," she said agreeing with me. "I like to make key lime pie when it's hot like it is today to cool me off, not to mention that it tastes good," she said with a slight giggle.

"Do you want something to drink," I asked turning toward her after putting the pie onto a small plate.

"No thanks. I'm not going to stay. I just wanted to bring that by before I go shopping. You want to come?"

There were a few more items I wanted to get before the baby came. I thought about the money Mama sent and looked over at Rodney. He looked at me and shrugged.

Kristen didn't miss the exchange. "Oh, I'm sorry. You probably want to spend some time with your husband."

"No, it's fine. He's going back to work in a little while. Let me change and put on something else. I'll come over when I'm done."

"I wouldn't think of it. It's too hot for you to be walking out there right now. Call me when you're ready and I'll stop by and pick you up."

I walked Kristen to the door and closed it behind her.

Rodney switched off the TV and got up to put his tray away. "I better get back," he said.

I went into the bedroom to change my clothes. Rodney entered a few minutes later. "Don't forget to starch and iron those khaki pants, I gotta go."

"Alright," I said as I continued dressing. The door closed behind him a few seconds later. By the time I got finished, I was almost out of breath. It took me forever to get dressed these days. The hardest part was putting on my sneakers. I usually tried to take them off without untying them so that I wouldn't have to bend over to tie them up.

Kristen and I decided to go to the shops on Riverside Drive. I rarely ventured into downtown Clarksville, so the trip was more of a sightseeing event for me. I was surprised by how warm it was outside. Kristen had the air conditioner on full blast.

We decided to go to Two Rivers Mall first to see if they had any good bargains. I was a little disappointed in how run down the mall was. Kristen told me about a new mall under construction on Wilma Rudolph Boulevard.

"I'm sure it will look a lot better than this," I said.

"Yeah, this one needs remodeling or something." As we walked toward the door, I suddenly had a craving for ice cream. "Do you think they have an ice cream shop in here?"

"I'm sure they have one somewhere. Let's walk down to the other end and see."

As soon as we turned around, I froze. I simply stared at the tall lanky man walking toward me. I wasn't able to turn around fast enough.

"Claudette. Is that you," he called out behind me.

I turned around slowly as Walter walked up to me and smiled. His smile vanished when he got a good look at my protruding belly.

"So, how have you been?"

"Fine," I finally managed to croak.

I introduced him to Kristen and prayed he would quickly be on his way.

"That's good to hear. So are you living here again?"

I nodded again. I was surprised that Francine had not told him that I had moved back to the area.

"There you are. I was looking all over for you," a whispery voice said behind me.

We all turned toward a slender young woman with brown curly hair walking toward us.

Walter held out his hand to her and introduced her. Claudette and Kristen this is my friend, April.

Kristen and I said hello to her in unison. I felt extremely awkward and wanted this gathering to end. "Well, we gotta get going. Nice to see you again Walter," I said before motioning to Kristen that I was ready to go.

"Yes, it was good seeing you again, Claudette. Take care of yourself."

I started walking as fast as my legs would carry me. "That Walter is cute," Kristen said when she caught up to me.

I didn't respond.

"You still want to get some ice cream?"

"I shook my head and kept walking."

"Are you alright Claudette?"

"Yeah, I'm fine," I lied.

We walked back to the car in silence. Kristen turned on the air conditioner as soon as she got the car started, but we were both perspiring heavily before the car cooled off.

"You don't have to tell me if you don't want to, but something happened back there to upset you. Is Walter an old fling?"

I looked at her sharply. "Why would you think that?"

"It was obvious that something was going on. I mean if you could have seen your face when you saw him."

"No, he's not an old fling. It almost got to that point, but it didn't.

Kristen looked at me quickly before looking back at the road. "Were you hurt by it?"

I didn't respond immediately.

"I'm sorry, Claudette. I shouldn't be prying."

"No, I wasn't hurt by it, but he was," I said somberly.

"Well, it looks like he has moved on." She glanced toward me and went on

I thought of how to change the subject. I didn't particularly want to talk about Walter or Rodney with Kristen. "I guess so," I said lamely.

"So do you want to find another ice-cream shop?"

"No, that's OK. I think the craving has passed."

"Are you sure?" Kristen asked.

"Yeah, I'm good. I have some at home anyway. Where do you want to go now?"

"Hey, do you want to go shopping in Nashville? I know my way around pretty good."

"Nashville? You go shopping all the way down there?"

Kristen laughed when she saw the expression on my face.

"Yeah, I do. Do you have to get back by a certain time?"

"What about your girls?"

"Brian has the day off. He is spending the day with them and giving me a break." She winked and laughed.

"Must be nice," I said. "I just need to get back in time to fix dinner. How long will we be gone?"

"Hmm… around 4 or 4:30? Will that give you enough time?"

"That should be fine. Let's go."

❧ *Chapter 20* ❧

Rodney had been right. The baby was a little boy, so there was no question what his name would be. We nicknamed him RJ. It was uncanny how much he favored his father, even at this early stage. RJ was the cutest baby I had ever seen and I couldn't wait for Mama to see him. The day that he was born was almost a blur to me. The labor pains were excruciating, but it did not compare to the anger I felt towards my husband.

I had gone into labor soon after Rodney left for work on the morning of July 20. I called his unit and he was nowhere to be found. Finally, I had to call Francine and ask her to come and take me to the hospital. He made it to the hospital four and a half hours later and I was in full blown labor. I was furious. He walked in looking disheveled and nervous.

"Hey, I went to the house for lunch and you were gone."

I ignored him as I held on tightly to the bed rail. He came to stand beside me and brushed my hair away from my face. "Do you want me to call the nurse," he asked anxiously.

I continued to ignore him until the contraction ended. I fell back on the pillow and tried to catch my breath. I could see Francine get up to leave.

I looked over at her. "Do you have to go?"

She eyed Rodney uneasily before looking at me. "I go in at noon. Now that your husband is here I'll give you two sometime alone. I'll check in on you later to see how things are going."

She left without bothering to speak to Rodney and he didn't' say anything to her.

"So how are things coming? Is it almost time?"

I glared at him angrily. "Where have you been? I called your unit almost five hours ago and they didn't know where you were."

He seemed surprised by my anger. "What do you mean, where

have I been? I was at work!"

"That's not what Sergeant McKenzie said!"

"I don't care what McKenzie said. He doesn't work in our office, so he wouldn't know if I was there or not. I had to go to the motor pool to check on some parts for our trucks. That's where I've been all this time." His eyes were flashing with fury.

"They said they looked for you and couldn't find you," I lashed out at him.

Rodney rolled his eyes up at the ceiling. "Didn't you just hear what I said," he replied through clenched teeth. "I was at the motor pool. Obviously, he wouldn't have been able to find me."

I glared angrily at him before grabbing the rails again. The doctor stuck his head in through the curtains just as the contraction began leveling off.

"Mrs. Jackson, I want to check you again to see how things are coming and then we are going to get you hooked up to a fetal monitor so we can monitor the intensity of your contractions. He looked over at Rodney. "Are you the proud papa?"

Rodney's scowl quickly left his face as he nodded and shook the doctor's hand. "Yes sir."

The doctor checked me quickly and asked the nurse to give me something to help ease the pain, but I didn't feel it. I went to sleep until the next excruciating pain hit me. Things continued like that for almost two hours before I heard the doctor say that they were taking me into the delivery room.

Things happened quickly after that and I felt as though I was in a daze. It was hard to focus on the different voices I heard around me commanding me to keep pushing. Twenty minutes later, I heard a baby crying and knew that it was finally over.

Rodney called Mama and his parents moments after the baby was born. He said he could tell that Mama was crying on the other end. I called her as soon as I got home from the hospital and tried to describe everything about her new grandson. She told me about all of the adorable little things that she had just mailed for him.

"Dee-Dee, they got the cutest little baby clothes now. Pearl had to practically drag me out of the store. Some of the things might be a bit big, but he'll grow into 'em."

"Thanks Mama." We talked for another twenty minutes about the baby.

"Alright, let me let you go. I know how valuable your time is now. Babies don't sleep long." She chuckled softly before hanging up.

My life changed dramatically after the birth of the baby. Getting up with him was my job without question. Rodney didn't even hear me when I crawled out of bed. I was tired all the time. Having time to do my hair and nails was a luxury. Every minute of every day was planned around the baby.

Rodney seemed proud to be a father. He bragged to his parents about how much the baby looked like him when his mother called a few days after I came home from the hospital. He talked to both of his parents for a few minutes before handing the phone to me.

"My mom wants to talk to you."

Why on earth did his mother want to speak to me, I wondered.
"Hello."

"Hello Dee-Dee. I just wanted to see how you were doing. I'm glad to see that everything is working out fine."

I knew that she was referring to my marriage, but I chose to ignore it. "Yes, the baby is doing fine and eating quite a bit," I said.

"I don't doubt that. His father is a big eater. Send some pictures as soon as you can," she said before ending the conversation.

I gave the phone back to Rodney so that he could say his good-byes. He talked briefly with his mother before hanging up.

Rodney was still fast asleep when I decided to get up early to wash my hair this morning. It wasn't a surprise that he was sleeping in. He had gotten in late again last night. I was so tired that I hadn't bothered to look at the clock when he crawled into bed. His behavior was starting to annoy me. He had been coming in later and later and he always reeked of alcohol.

By the time he walked into the kitchen, I had been up for two hours. I had left a plate of sausage, bacon and eggs in the oven for him.

"We need to go and get the baby some more pampers," I exclaimed as soon as he came into the kitchen and sat down at the table.

He looked at me with a raised eyebrow. "I just bought pampers a couple days ago."

"That was over a week ago. He's almost out."

"I'll get some later. I need to take my boots to the shop to see if they can replace the heel anyway."

It was obvious that I would not be accompanying him to the

store. I had been stuck in this house for over two weeks and I was hoping that this Saturday I would be able to get out of the house for a bit.

"Why don't I go get it? I need to get out for some fresh air and I want to get a few things from the store."

Rodney seemed surprised by my suggestion. "You just had a baby Dee-Dee. Isn't it too early for you to be out of the house?"

His question annoyed me even though my mother said the same thing every time she called.

"Don't try to be out there in the streets too early Dee-Dee. You don't want to get sick. Take time to heal."

I didn't understand how I was going to get sick as hot as it was outside, but I was not going to argue with Mama. I did have a doctor's appointment next week and I was sure that the doctor would say that it was safe to be out and about.

"I don't think it's too early. I have to leave the house on Tuesday when we take the baby for his check-up."

"Well why not wait until the doctor says it's OK" he asked sarcastically.

"Rodney, I don't see how two days is going to make any difference," I said, upset by his tone of voice.

"Write a list of the things you need and I will get them." He turned his attention back to the show he was watching.

His attitude infuriated me. I went into our room to get a load of clothes ready for the laundry hoping that RJ would sleep a little while longer. As I sorted through the clothes, a tiny piece of paper fell onto the carpet. I frowned as I looked at the folded paper before checking to see what it was. *Here is my new number, Stephanie.*

I reread the message again and stared at the phone number. I was furious. I stormed into the living room. "Who is Stephanie?"

Rodney was caught off guard as he held his fork in mid air. "What?"

"Who is Stephanie?"

"I don't know."

I walked toward him and threw the paper on the table in front of him. I folded my hands across my chest waiting for him to answer my question.

He sighed and put the plate on the table before picking up the scrap of paper. He threw it back onto the table and refused to look at me.

"I don't know who that is."

Here we go again, I thought. "You do know who it is? How would the note get in your pocket if you didn't know her?"

Rodney sat back and folded his arms. His eyes became cold as steel. "I already told you that I don't know who that is. Now drop it!"

I was incensed as memories of his denials about Collins flooded my mind. "No, I'm not going through this again with you. If you want someone else, then you can have her."

I went back into the bedroom and slammed the door behind me. I threw myself onto the bed and refused to let a tear fall from my eye. It wasn't long before I heard the baby whimpering in the bassinet behind me. It was his feeding time and there was no point in trying to get him to go back to sleep. I reached for him gently and tried to head off the wails that would surely come in a matter of minutes if I didn't move quickly.

Rodney came in and stood in the doorway staring angrily at me. "Look, I told you I don't know who that is. I am not foolin' around on you if that's what you think. That note you found could have come from anywhere."

I ignored him as I continued to get RJ ready for his feeding.

"Do you hear me talking to you Dee-Dee?"

When I did not respond he abruptly turned to leave. A few seconds later, I heard the front door slam behind him. As I fed the baby, I let the tears flow kicking myself for letting him do this to me again.

After I fed the baby, I changed his pamper and watched over him tenderly before he drifted off to sleep again. Normally, I tried to nap when he did, but there was no way I'd be able to go to sleep right now. I went back into the living room to look for the scrap of paper. It was nowhere to be found. *Humph, you don't know her alright!*

I moped around for most of the day beating myself up for allowing Rodney to make a fool of me yet again. All of the sacrifices had been made by me. I had given up my job, car, and college in hopes that my wayward husband would change. I had long since given up on the idea of us going to see a marriage counselor. Rodney always changed the subject whenever I brought it up.

"We don't need to go and see no shrink," he would reply disdainfully.

"It can't hurt. There are lots of people who go to marriage

counselors," I answered.

"They go because they have lots of problems in their marriage. I don't see anything wrong with our marriage to tell you the truth."

He usually had something similar to say when I mentioned looking for a church. "All those people going to church ain't nothing but a bunch of hypocrites and those preachers just want your money," he quickly protested. He always came up with one excuse after another.

I pounded the pillow in fury as I thought about the hopelessness of my situation. He was probably with her right now. The phone rang beside me and startled me.

"Hello." There was no response on the other end. "Hello," I repeated.

The person on the other end hung up. *How could I have been so stupid?*

The phone rang again and I snatched it up. "Hello," I shouted angrily.

"Hey, it's me Kristin. Is everything OK?"

"Hey. Yes everything is fine. Did you call a minute ago?"

"No. Why?"

"Somebody called and hung up on me. I'm sorry for yelling at you that way."

"I completely understand. It upsets me when that happens to me."

There was a moment of awkward silence before Kristen piped in. "Oh, I was calling to check on you and the baby. How are things coming along? Do you need anything?"

Kristen had been so helpful since I came home from the hospital. She had brought over several pans of prepared meals, for which I was truly grateful.

"No. We're fine. I appreciate everything that you've done so far."

"It's no bother. Are you sure? I made some lasagna and decided to make an extra pan just in case. I was planning to bring it over in a few minutes, but decided to give you a call to see if you needed anything else before I come over."

There was no way that I would be able to repay Kristen for all that she had done. It was good that Rodney didn't object to our friendship like he did with Francine. She had come over a couple weeks ago to bring a gift for RJ when I told her that Rodney would be working late.

"I'm not going to stay long. You know how your husband feels about me." It was hard to maintain our friendship with her and Rodney at odds with one another.

"You are welcome anytime."

Francine looked at me with a raised eyebrow. "Yeah right, that's what you say. We would have World War III going on in here if he walked through those doors right now."

We chatted for a while as she held the baby.

"He is adorable Claudette. I hate to say it, but this child is the spitting image of your husband."

I rolled my eyes. "Yeah, I know."

I always enjoyed my chats with Francine and I often wondered if she thought that I was a fool for getting back together with Rodney after all that she and Walter had done to get me away from him a little over a year ago.

I pounded the pillow again before the doorbell rang. *It must be Kristen.*

True to her word, Kristen marched in with Bria and Bryann right behind her. "They have been begging me to let them come with me to see the baby. Do you mind?"

They flashed their adorable little smiles at me before waving.

"Not at all. Why don't you have a seat? I'll go get him." RJ must have known that he was about to be the center of attention. He was wide awake and all smiles as soon as I picked him up.

Kristen reached for him as soon as I walked into the living room. "He is the cutest little thing Claudette."

The girls swarmed in and played with him as their mother held him on her lap. "Can I hold him," they begged repeatedly.

"Maybe when he gets a little older," Kristen said.

It was hard to keep from smiling as I watched them playing with my son. We all turned to look when the door opened minutes later and Rodney walked in.

He looked at Kristen and nodded. "How you doing?"

"Hey, the girls were begging to come over and see your beautiful baby."

Rodney smiled and looked over at me. He plopped a large bag of pampers in the loveseat.

Kristen glanced over at me and gave RJ a kiss on his forehead. "Well little guy, we are going to head on home and give you a break."

"But we just got here," the twins protested.

"You don't have to leave," Rodney said as he looked at them.

"Yeah, I need to head on back. Brian is probably wondering what in the world is keeping me. I told him I would only be gone a few minutes." She laughed and handed the baby to me.

"Thanks again for the lasagna."

"Not a problem. I put some garlic rolls in there too."

I smiled. "Thanks."

As soon as they left, Rodney looked at me. "Washburn and his wife are coming over later. She wants to see the baby."

I nodded. I liked Washburn's wife and enjoyed their company when they came over, but today was not the best day for company. I quickly gathered the babies' things and went into the bedroom to watch TV until they got here.

It wasn't long before the door bell rang and I heard Rodney greeting Washburn. I gathered up the baby and went into the living room. Nora rushed toward me as soon as she saw me.

"Oh, Honey look. Isn't he the sweetest little thing," she exclaimed over her shoulders.

"May I hold him?"

I nodded and handed the baby over to her.

"How you doing Claudette?" Washburn said as he walked toward me. "We bought this for the baby." He handed me a wrapped gift.

"I'm fine. Thank you for the gift."

Nora cuddled the baby gently and moved slowly to the sofa. What did you name him?"

We named him after Rodney, but we call him RJ," I said as I opened the gift. It was a little blue sleeper with matching booties and a bib. "Thank you, this will come in handy."

"Thank you."

"He is so cute, Dee-Dee.

"That's because he looks just like me," Rodney added.

Nora looked at me and rolled her eyes. "It figures that he would say that."

"Well he does," Rodney repeated.

Nora laughed. "Yes, he looks like you. I guess it could be worse."

Washburn laughed and slapped his leg.

"I can't wait until we have kids," Nora said as she put her finger in RJ's hand and smiled when he grasped it tightly.

"Alright, don't get any ideas over there," Washburn said to her jokingly.

"That's a good idea. What are you waiting on man," Rodney said waiting on Washburn to respond.

Washburn shook his head. "We need to wait until the finances are right. Besides, she got me to take care of right now."

"Would you like something to drink?" I asked.

"Yeah, man you want something?" Rodney gave Washburn a knowing look.

"A Coke for me please." I'm sure I'll be the one driving home," Nora said as she looked up at Rodney and Washburn and shook her head.

Washburn laughed. "You know how it is Baby." He looked at Rodney and the two of them started laughing again.

I went into the kitchen to get the drink for Nora. She followed me and sat at the table.

"We might as well sit in here at the table so we can talk for a bit. So how are you feeling?"

"Everything's fine. I'm ready to get out of this house though. It's hard being cooped up in here all the time."

Nora nodded. "That must be tough."

Rodney came into the kitchen and got a beer for Washburn and fixed a drink for himself.

Nora looked at me and shook her head. "It's a good thing he won't be driving nowhere after all that stuff he poured in there," she said when he went back into the living room.

"It seems to be a habit for them now when they get off in the afternoons," I said tersely.

Nora gave me a puzzled look. "You mean he drinks like that during the week?"

"Yeah, when they all go out together after work," I replied. "Don't Washburn go with them?"

Nora raised her eyebrow and frowned. "No. They only do that on Thursdays when they have happy hour at the club, but Tony hasn't been going with them lately."

I sat there thinking about how many times Rodney had gotten in late over the past couple weeks and frowned. He had stayed out late almost every night except Monday.

Nora put her hand over mine and whispered. "Look, I don't want to be the one to start something between you and your man, so maybe he's going out with other guys. I just know that my husband isn't going with them."

I looked at her and gave her a half smile before blurting out, "So who is Stephanie?"

Nora eyes registered her surprise as she searched my face. She glanced in the living room quickly to see if the men had heard me.

"Why do you ask?"

"Because I think you know who she is." I was amazed by this sudden boldness that had overtaken me.

Nora looked down and brushed away imaginary lint from RJ's bib. She looked up at me and paused.

"Claudette, I really think you should be asking your husband that question."

I could tell that I had made her uncomfortable, but I didn't care. I was getting angry because it was obvious that something was going on behind my back and everybody knew about it except me.

"So you're not going to tell me. If it were you would you want to know?"

Nora sighed and pleaded with her eyes for me not to pursue the issue. "It's not that. It's just that I don't want to be the one starting problems here," she said before looking at Rodney to be sure he couldn't hear her. "What did your husband say when you asked about her?"

"He told me he didn't know who she was."

Nora dropped her head for a second. "Well, I guess you just have to take his word that he doesn't know who she is then."

I sat back in my chair and thought about what had just occurred. It was obvious that Nora knew something and she did not want to tell me because she didn't want Rodney or Washburn to come down on her about it.

"So how would you handle this if it were you," I asked.

Nora looked down at RJ who had fallen asleep by this time. "Claudette, it's obvious that you are suspicious about something or you wouldn't be asking me all these questions. If I were you and I thought something was going on with my husband, I would try to find out for myself."

"That's exactly what I'm trying to do," I said angrily.

Nora squirmed uncomfortably.

"I mean you need to check things out and show up when he tells you he's going somewhere to see if he's telling you the truth."

"And how am I supposed to do that if he has the car?" I suddenly remembered how Rodney had tried to convince me to sell my car before we came back up here. It all worked out perfectly for him. The only time I could go anywhere was when he went with me or if he was out in the field.

"I don't know."

"That's why I need help. I'm stuck here in the house all the time. There is no way for me to find out on my own.

Nora nodded. "I know that has to be hard especially with a new baby, but if you really want to know what's going on with your husband, you need to be the one to find out for yourself. I don't want to be in the middle of it. I'm sorry."

This was pointless. I had no right to do this to her. Rodney was my problem, not hers.

"No. I'm sorry. I had no right to try to pressure you like that. That was wrong. I've just been under a lot of stress lately."

Nora looked at me sadly. "The real question is, even if you found out something, what are you going to do about it? What's the point in knowing if nothing is going to change? You would be better off not knowing. That's just how I feel about it."

We sat there lost in our thoughts until Washburn walked into the kitchen startling us both.

"Why do you two look so serious in here?"

Nora and I looked up at him and smiled.

"Are you about ready Babe?"

She nodded and patted RJ's head. "He's a sweetheart. We need to have a baby soon."

Washburn held his head back and laughed. "See that's why I need to keep you away from babies."

I got up and gently lifted RJ from her lap trying not to wake him. I took him into the room and lay him in the bassinet. By the time I came back into the living room, Washburn and Nora were standing at the door.

"It was good seeing you again Claudette. Hopefully the next time I see you, I will have some good news of my own."

Washburn shook his head and laughed. "Alright, we need to be going. It's getting late. Bye."

Rodney and I said our good-byes.

As soon as the door closed behind them, I turned to go back into the bedroom. There was no way that I could bring up Stephanie right now or he would know that Nora had said something to me about it. I would just have to take her advice and find out for myself. *Sooner or later, the truth is going to come out.*

Chapter 21

T hings got progressively worse for Rodney and me. We barely spoke to each other anymore. I pretended to be asleep when he came in late and he seemed content to leave it that way. One night when he came in reeking of alcohol, I got up, took a blanket out of the closet and went into the living room to sleep on the sofa.

Within minutes Rodney was standing over me. "Why are you sleeping out here? Is something wrong with our bed?"

"I would rather sleep here," I said tersely.

"Come back to bed, Dee-Dee."

"I'm fine out here," I said refusing to budge.

"Look woman, I don't know why you acting like this, but we got a bed. There is no reason for you to sleep out here." He grabbed my arm roughly and pulled me up from the sofa.

I cried out in pain and tried to push him away from me.

Rodney snatched the blanket away from me and pushed me toward the bedroom. "I've had enough of this Dee-Dee!"

"Enough of what?" I demanded as I turned to face him. "You had enough of sleeping around with anything in a skirt?"

Rodney let out a short laugh. "So that's what this is all about. You still trying to accuse me of something."

"You know that it's the truth."

"Then prove it. Who am I messing around with?"

"Stephanie! You made sure that I would be stuck in this house without a car so that I wouldn't be able to prove it. The only time I get to go anywhere is if you take me, in the meantime, you come and go as you please." I was amazed by my words and shocked that I was choosing to stand up to Rodney to his face.

"We already been through all that and you still can't prove it," he said snidely. You only **think** you got something on me, but you don't."

"Yeah, that's what you said about Teresa Collins too."

Even though I couldn't see Rodney's eyes clearly, I knew that they were now hard as coals. I could sense the fury that was beginning to rage on the inside of him, but I didn't care.

"If you're finished we can go back to bed. Let's go!" The annoyance in his voice was unmistakable.

I refused to budge.

Seconds later I felt the sharp sting across my face. I moved backwards and tripped on the blanket.

Rodney reached down and tried to yank me up again. I pushed his hand away angrily. I was like a crazed woman and it didn't matter to me what he did to me at this point. He had lied to me again and I was sure that his late nights were spent with someone else even if I couldn't prove it.

I stared up at him as he waited for me to get up. As soon as I did, he hit me again. I cried out and fell backwards onto the sofa. "I'm not going to keep playing this game with you Dee-Dee," he said through clenched teeth.

Rodney grabbed my arm and pulled me off the sofa. The pain shot through me and left me breathless for a second. He pushed me toward the bedroom door. When I got into the bedroom, he swung me around to face him. "Hopefully, we are through with this conversation unless there is something else you need to say."

Without thinking, I pushed him angrily and he hit his back against the door. Rodney rushed toward me and grabbed me by the throat. I kept trying to break free of his grip, but he held me fast.

"Woman if you ever come at me like that again, I will kill you," he hissed out at me before pushing me down roughly on the bed. The commotion woke the baby and he started to cry. I got up from the bed and rushed into the bathroom. I locked the door behind me and sat on the commode. I could hear Rodney in the other room trying to soothe the baby. I got up and washed my face before looking in the mirror.

My face was red where Rodney had hit me and I could see his prints on my throat. RJ continued to wail loudly and Rodney could not calm him down. I came out of the bathroom and took the baby from him and sat down on the bed to feed him. I was still shaking pretty bad, but I did not feel afraid.

"Look, I didn't mean to hit you, but you made me do it Dee-Dee."

I kept my eyes fixed on the floor in front of me. "I'm tired of you lying to me Rodney."

He threw his hands up angrily. "What am I lying about? I told you that I am not messing around on you."

"And I guess that's why you stay out late almost every night and come home smelling like a liquor factory."

"No. I go to happy hour with my friends. We have a few drinks, that's all."

"What friends? The only night they have happy hour is on Thursday's. You have been coming home late almost every night.

He laughed and I could tell that he didn't know how to respond to what I had just said.

"I'm telling you the truth Dee-Dee. Nothing is going on."

I didn't bother to respond to him.

"Why don't you believe me?"

"That's what you said about Collins, remember!"

"Don't keep throwing Collins up in my face," he said furiously. That's over and done with. You need to let the past stay in the past!"

RJ began to whimper softly as we continued to shout back and forth to each other. I tried to get him settled down, but it wasn't working. I got up and paced the floor patting him gently on the back to get him to calm down.

Rodney left the room as I continued to comfort the baby. It took a few minutes, but I finally got him to settle down and go back to sleep. I knew that it was going to be a long night for me. It was difficult to get to sleep when I was upset with Rodney and with a new baby; I needed all of the sleep I could get.

I crawled into the bed and tried to force myself to sleep. I pretended to be asleep when Rodney came back into the room. He peeked in the bassinet at the baby before coming to bed. Thankfully, he left me alone when he got in the bed. It wasn't long before he was snoring loudly. I lay there for hours trying to figure out what I was going to do. Nora's words came rushing back to me. *"What's the point in knowing if nothing's going to change?"* There was no point in trying to force myself to sleep. It wasn't working. I needed a plan. Here I was in the same situation as before thinking that things would change for us. But things hadn't changed, they had gotten worse.

I'm never going to get to sleep. I got up quietly and slipped on my robe. I tiptoed into the kitchen and reached into the cabinet and got the bottle that Rodney kept hidden under the counter and poured a drink. I stood there looking at the glass and contemplated whether or not to drink it. Seconds later, I tried to catch my breath as the fiery liquid raced down my throat. After I had recovered, I made my way back into the bedroom.

What seemed like minutes later, I was being shaken awake. "What in the world is wrong with you? The baby is awake and I need to go to work. Get up!" I glanced over at the clock and groaned. I didn't even hear it go off.

I quickly got up and staggered into the bathroom. I jumped into the shower hoping the cold water would give me a jolt to make me snap out of my stupor. A few minutes later, Rodney stuck his head in the bathroom. I could hear RJ screaming at the top of his lungs.

"Hurry up woman. I gotta go and RJ is ready to eat!"

I dried off as fast as I could and wrapped my robe around me tightly. I was still feeling light headed, but things weren't as fuzzy as before. It didn't take long to get RJ fed and bathed and before long, he was nodding off to sleep.

I lay him in the bed with me and before long I had fallen back to sleep. A few hours later, I awoke and got up to get myself something to eat. I felt miserable and my head was pounding. I dressed and cleaned up the kitchen. It wouldn't be long before RJ would be up for another feeding.

My day went by in a blur. I tried not to think about last night. It was too painful to think about my situation with Rodney. I knew deep down inside that something was going on, but he was right. I had no proof, only a gut feeling. Rodney continued to stay out late and came home smelling like stale liquor mixed with perfume.

Night after night, after putting the baby to bed, I would force myself to drink the strong drink hoping that it would dull the pain and help me forget about my problems. On one particular night, I lay there not feeling a thing. *Maybe I didn't have enough,* I thought to myself. I got up to go back into the kitchen to try again, but as I stood there staring at the bottle in my hand; I felt a tug within my heart that filled me with sadness.

I began to cry bitter tears and fell on my knees with my face in my hands. *God, I'm sorry. This is not who I am. Please forgive. If this is not the man for me, get me out of this and show me how to make a life for my baby. Jesus, help me. I don't know what do.*

I cried until I was spent. Minutes later, a strange sense of peace overshadowed me.

I began to cry again, but I was no longer sad. I felt relieved. As I sat there on the kitchen floor wondering about what had just happened, the phone rang. It scared me. I looked at the clock and wondered who would be calling at 12:20 in the morning. I thought about Mama. The last time we had gotten a call this late at night, she had fallen down the steps. *Oh, God, please let Mama be alright.*

The phone rang a second time before I got up to answer it. "Hello."

"Mrs. Jackson, this is Blanchfield Army Hospital calling about your husband PFC. Rodney Jackson."

My heart dropped to the floor and I could not speak.

"Mrs. Jackson are you there?"

"Ah, yes. What's wrong with my husband," I asked weakly.

"He was in an accident. He's alive, but we need to have you come over here as soon as possible."

I was frozen with fear. The caller repeated herself to make sure I had heard her. "Yes. I will be there shortly."

I hung up the phone. But how was I going to get there? Rodney had the car. *Francine.* The phone rang several times before she finally answered.

"Hello," she answered groggily.

"Francine. It's me. Rodney's been in an accident and I don't have a way to get to the hospital. Can you come and take me over there?"

"What, is he alright?"

"I guess so, but they need me to come."

"OK, let me get dressed and I will be over there."

I hung up the phone and raced into the bedroom and froze in my tracks. What about RJ? Oh, God, what am I going to do now? His car seat was in our car, so I couldn't take him with me.

There was no way that I could take the baby with me. If we got stopped without a car seat, I would get Francine in a whole lot of trouble. Maybe Francine would stay here with the baby and let me drive her car, I thought. *I've been drinking, what if got stopped?* Suddenly I remembered Kristen. I'll call Kristen. I went back into the kitchen to dial her number. I hated getting people up at this time of night, but I was desperate.

Brian answered the phone. I told him what had happened and he immediately put her on the phone.

"Just drop him off over here. I'll keep him for you," Kristen said quickly.

"Are you sure?"

"Yes, of course, bring him over here."

I went back into the room to get dressed. I packed a bag for RJ and took him into the living room to wait on Francine. I was a nervous wreck. Thankfully, the doorbell rang a few minutes later.

I rushed to the door to let Francine in. "Girl, I got here as fast as I could. You ready?" She looked at the baby and stopped. "Do you have a car seat for the baby?"

"I'm taking him to Kristen. She's going to keep him until I get back."

I grabbed the baby and his bag before following Francine out of the house. We pulled into Kristen's driveway two minutes later. She was watching for us through the window.

I got out and hurried to the door. Kristen was already at the door waiting to take the baby. "I got him. You go on now. He'll be alright. Call me when you know something."

"I will," I said and ran back to the car praying that my husband was going to be OK.

❧ *Chapter 22* ❧

Francine tried to stay within the speed limit on the way to the hospital, but I knew she was pushing it a bit. Neither one of us spoke on the way. We pulled into the hospital's parking lot a few minutes later. I quickly got out of the car and rushed into the Emergency Room.

I gave the receptionist my name and told them about the call I had gotten. Francine quietly stood beside me.

"Have a seat Mrs. Jackson and I will let the doctors know that you are here."

I stood there staring at the woman, surprised that she was not going to take me in to see him immediately.

Francine grabbed my arm and pulled me toward a row of chairs. A few people were scattered around the room, but I barely looked at them. "Come on, those are the standard procedures. They'll come and get you as soon as they're done."

We sat down and waited. It wasn't long before I heard my name being called. I stood up as a young man walked toward me and held out his hand. He looked like he may have been of Indian descent.

"Mrs. Jackson. I'm Doctor Singh. I have been caring for your husband. Let me calm your fears. Your husband will be fine. He has a fractured skull."

I gasped and covered my mouth with my hands.

The doctor put his hand on my shoulder. "I know that sounds frightening, but it's a simple linear fracture. We initially thought that he may have had some tissue damage beneath the bone, but it appears that he does not, so we will not have to go in to do any repairs. It should heal nicely on its own. He also has a few broken ribs that will take about two months to heal. We will give him some pain medication to help him manage the pain. We are going to keep him overnight for observation, but if everything else checks out, he will be released by tomorrow afternoon. Do you have any questions for me?"

"How did this happen?"

The doctor hesitated for a moment. "As I understand it, alcohol may have contributed to the accident causing the driver to lose control of the car. Your husband was thrown out of the vehicle."

I stood there trying to understand it all, yet thankful that his injuries weren't life threatening.

"Would you like me to take you to see him now?"

I nodded and followed him as he walked through the double doors. He walked into a tiny little room and pulled the curtains back for me. Rodney was sleeping but he had a large bandage on the side of his face and his body was wrapped in bandages from the waist up to his chest.

I walked over to the bed and reached for his hand.

"I'll leave you here for a few minutes if you'd like to sit with him," Dr. Singh said before leaving the room.

I caressed Rodney's arm gently as the tears rolled down my cheeks. A few minutes later, the curtain was pulled back and two Military Police officer's came in. They looked at me and nodded. "Are you Mrs. Jackson?"

I frowned before responding. "Yes."

"How are you ma'am," the officer closest to me said as he looked back at Rodney.

"I'm fine."

He nodded. "We'll come back later when your husband is awake. We just have a few questions we'd like him to answer about the driver of the car."

"What do you mean? Wasn't my husband driving the car?"

"One of the officers looked down at his notes. "No ma'am."

"That doesn't make any sense then. Rodney is not one to let just anybody drive his car. Who was driving?"

The two officers exchanged glances before looking back at me. I got a funny feeling in the pit of my stomach and knew that I didn't want to know the answer to that question.

"Who was driving our car?" I repeated.

"Well, ma'am we are not showing that the car is registered to your husband. He was simply the passenger."

Now I was really lost for words. "Then whose car was it?"

The officer looked down at the pad again. "Ma'am, we really think it would be best if we came back when your husband wakes up. He can probably answer these questions a lot better than we can."

The two officers nodded and walked out of the room.

I stood there staring at Rodney as I thought about Dr. Singh's comment, "...*alcohol was a contributing factor causing the driver to lose control of the car. Your husband was thrown out of the vehicle.*"

Who was the driver and what had happened to him or was it her? I suddenly felt weak. I walked out of the room just as Dr. Singh walked by. I decided to test my hunch.

"Doctor, can you tell me how Stephanie is doing?"

He looked at me as if he didn't know who I was referring to. "Stephanie?" he repeated.

"Yes, the driver of the car that my husband was riding in."

He nodded. "Oh, Ms. Phillips, do you know her?"

I nodded.

"Although I cannot give you specific details about her, she is holding her own right now and we are hoping for the best." Doctor Singh glanced in the direction of the room near the double doors we entered to come back here. "Is there anything we can get for you Mrs. Jackson?"

"No. Thank you Doctor."

I stood watching him as he walked down the hall toward the nurse's desk. I looked at the curtain where he had looked earlier and knew that Stephanie was in that room. I went back into Rodney's room and stood there staring at him as he slept. All of the sympathy that I had felt earlier was gone. I was filled with rage and I wanted to drag him out of that bed.

I left the room to go back into the sitting room. When I reached the last room on the right, I glanced over at the nurse's station. There was only one nurse sitting there and she had her back turned. I quickly pulled the curtain back and entered the tiny area. I was not prepared for what I would see.

The young woman in front of me had her entire head completely bandaged. I could tell that she was extremely light skinned. The only things showing were her eyelids, nose and mouth. She had all kinds of tubes and machines attached to her. I quickly left the room and went into the waiting area with Francine.

Francine woke up as soon as I sat down. "How's Rodney?"

"He's going to be OK," I said trying to hold back the pent up emotions inside of me.

"So the doctors feel he's going to be alright," Francine asked.

I nodded trying to think of how much I wanted to share with her.

A few minutes later an older couple rushed through the doors. The woman had tears streaking down her face. The man grabbed the woman's hand as they hurried over to the desk.

"Ma'am we got a call that our granddaughter was here," I heard him say.

"Sir, what's your granddaughter's name?"

"Stephanie Phillips," the woman said quickly.

The receptionist stood up and spoke to the man. "Sir, I will let the doctor know that you are here. Would you please have a seat and we will call for you."

My eyes followed the couple as they huddled closely and came near to where Francine and I were sitting. It was hard not to feel sorry for them seeing how upset they were about their granddaughter. The husband ushered his wife to a seat and he remained standing.

The woman was still very beautiful in spite of her age. It was clear that Stephanie had her grandmother's complexion. The grandfather was a little darker with curly gray hair. As I looked at the two of them, it was hard to remain angry with their granddaughter. After all, I was married to Rodney. He was the one who had betrayed me, not Stephanie. I said a silent prayer that she would pull through and be OK.

I turned to Francine. "I don't even know if I want to hang around here."

Francine looked at me and frowned.

"What's wrong Claudette?"

"Mr. and Mrs. Phillips," I heard the receptionist call out behind me.

The couple hurried over to the desk. "Mr. Phillips, are Stephanie's parents on their way," the receptionist asked. I was sitting close enough to the desk, so that it was easy to hear what they were saying from where I was sitting.

"Stephanie is living with us so that she can finish college. Her mother is a soldier and she is stationed in Korea right now."

The receptionist wrote the information down quickly as a nurse approached the couple.

"So your daughter is in Korea, but she left Stephanie in your care," she repeated.

"We have the power of attorney," the grandfather said worriedly. "And she should have her ID card with her."

"Yes. We have her ID card sir. That's why the paramedics brought her here. We just needed to get some additional information," the nurse said. "I'll take you back to talk to the doctor now. Follow me please."

The couple held hands as they followed the nurse through the double doors.

I turned to Francine and told her the entire story, even about how I had been trying to get drunk at night in order to go to sleep.

Francine sighed and shook her head. "I don't know what to say Claudette. I know how much you wanted things to work out."

"Humph. It appears that I was the only one trying to make it work. I could kick myself."

"Well, at least you tried. It saddens me to think that you would try to turn yourself into an alcoholic to deal with this though. Claudette, you have that baby to think about. What if there was an emergency or something and you were lying up in the bed drunk? That baby needs both of his parents and at least one of them need to be in their right mind."

"I know." I told her what happened to me right before I got the call about Rodney. Francine it's just so weird.

"I don't know what it's going to take for you girl, but God is trying to tell you something. You better start listening."

I smiled. "I think the message is coming through loud and clear. I had a feeling that Rodney was messing around, but I couldn't prove it. I don't see how he can lie his way out of this one."

"Give him enough time and he'll think of something."

We both shook our head.

"So what do you want to do?"

I sighed heavily. "I need to find out where the car is, so that I can get around. I know this sounds cruel, but I don't want to be there when he gets home. The doctor says he'll be fine, so he should be able to care for himself."

"Did you call his parents?"

"No. I forgot all about that."

"There is a pay phone over there."

My eyes followed where she was pointing. I got up and went to the phone. It took me a few minutes to remember the Jackson's phone number. I looked at the clock on the wall. It was almost 2 a.m. *Maybe I should just wait and call them in the morning?* I debated back and forth and decided to call.

"Hello," Mr. Jackson answered.

"Mr. Jackson, this is Claudette. I'm sorry to call this late, but I wanted to let you and Mrs. Jackson know that Rodney was in an accident." I waited for his response.

"Is he alright?" I detected a slight bit of fear in his voice.

"Who is it Harold," I heard Mrs. Jackson ask in the background.

"It's Rodney's wife. She say he been in a car wreck."

"Oh my," she exclaimed. "Is everything OK?"

"Hold on Doretha. That's what I'm trying to find out," he said curtly.

I told Mr. Jackson everything that the doctor told me.

I heard him breathe a sigh of relief and pass the message on to Mrs. Jackson.

"Thanks for callin'. Let us know if anything changes," he said before hanging up.

I walked back over to Francine, but before I could sit down, the nurse who had taken the Phillips' to see Stephanie came up to me.

"Mrs. Jackson, your husband is awake. We told him that you were here and he wants to see you." I nodded and looked at Francine. She gave me a knowing look and nodded her head.

I followed the nurse. As I walked by Stephanie's area, I could hear her grandmother talking to her.

"Come on Baby. Wake up! Grammy's here. Come on. Open your eyes Steffie." When the nurse pulled back the curtain I walked in and stood at the foot of the bed. My husband looked into my eyes and smiled.

"Hey Babe."

I just stood there without responding.

"You can go up closer the nurse said behind me. I'll just pull the curtains and give you two a little time together while we get his room ready upstairs."

I moved closer to him and continued to stare at him. He held out his hand and reached for me. "Come here. Why you looking all scared? I'm going to be alright."

Rodney grabbed my hand when I moved closer. "Where's the baby?"

"I left him with Kristen," I mumbled. "Francine brought me

here."

"Good. I'm a little banged up, but the doctor says I should be fine in a couple months."

"That's good. It could have been worse."

Rodney nodded.

"Where is our car," I asked calmly.

Rodney looked at me for a second and I could tell that he knew that I knew about Stephanie. He turned his eyes away and remained silent.

"I need to be able to get around, so I need you to tell me where the car is."

"Dee-Dee, listen to me. I know what you think, but you're wrong."

"Rodney, I don't want to talk about that right now. Just tell me where the car is, so Francine can take me by there to get it."

He turned to look at me. "Do you know where the club is on Ringgold Road?"

I gave him a blank stare. "I'm sure Francine knows where it is."

"The car is in the parking lot in the back of the club."

I turned to leave.

"Dee-Dee wait, I need you to listen to me."

"I called your parents and told them about the accident and that you were going to be OK," I said over my shoulders and walked out of the room.

I walked past the nurse's station and back into the waiting room. Francine had gone back to sleep. I nudged her gently.

Francine jumped. "Oh, girl, I must have nodded off again."

"I'm ready, but I need a favor. Do you know of a club on Ringgold Road?"

Francine frowned. "I think I do. Why?"

"That's where the car is. So if you could take me by there to get it, you can go straight home from there."

"Sure." Francine grabbed her purse before she stood up and stretched.

We found the car with no problem. Francine waited for me to get in and get it started. She blew the horn at me as she drove off. By the time I got to Kristen's house, it was almost 3:30 a.m. I tapped on the door lightly to avoid waking up the entire family. Kristen came to the door a few minutes later.

"Hey. Come on in. I put some blankets on the floor and made a little bed down here for RJ and me. How's your husband?"

"He's going to be alright." I told her what the doctor said and thanked her for watching the baby for me.

"No problem at all. What about the car? Is it drivable?"

"Yes. The car is fine. He was riding with someone else."

"Oh, well at least you'll have transportation."

I nodded as I reached down to get RJ. Kristen grabbed his bag and walked me to the door. She waited at the door as I got the baby into the car seat. I waved when I walked around the car and got into the driver's seat. Kristen waved and closed the door behind her.

When I got home, I put RJ in the bed with me and cried myself to sleep.

❧ *Chapter 23* ❧

M y mind was made up by the time I got up the next morning. I had gotten very little sleep as I thought about my situation. There was no point in waiting to put my plan in to motion. The first thing I did was to call Washburn and ask him to pick Rodney up from the hospital. He was stunned to learn about the accident and assured me that he would be there when he was released.

Next, I called Francine and told her of my plan to get a bus ticket and go back home to South Carolina before Rodney came home. She talked me out of taking the bus and told me I should fly home instead. I had never been on a plane before, so it took a lot of prodding on her part.

"Claudette, you really need to think about this. You have a newborn and that is a very long trip. Why don't you see if you can get a flight home? You'll be there by this afternoon. You could be on that bus for more than fifteen hours."

After giving her idea some considerable thought, I called the airport to check on flights to Charleston. Francine didn't have to go to work until three o'clock in the afternoon, so she was able to drive me to the airport in Nashville. I was a nervous wreck about flying, but Francine would not let up on me. I did agree that the long hours of being on a bus with a baby would be difficult.

The earliest flight wouldn't be leaving until three o'clock in the afternoon. Francine had to go to work at 3:00, so she planned to take us early and drop us off. That meant that I would have to wait around for a couple hours, but that was still better than taking the bus. Money for the ticket wouldn't be a problem either. I had three hundred dollars saved up, but I decided to go by the bank to get another hundred out just in case.

I called Kristen to let her know that I was leaving. She suspected that I was having problems in my marriage, so she wasn't too surprised.

"I am really going to miss you Claudette," she said sadly.

"I'll miss you too. You've been a good friend."

"Make sure you take care of that baby. He is so sweet."

"I will," I promised before hanging up.

When we got to the airport, Francine made sure that my bags were checked properly and helped me find the right terminal before she left. I was grateful for her help because all of this was very new to me. It was hard to say goodbye to her, but we both knew that this was for the best.

I was shaking pretty bad when we boarded the plane. The flight attendants were very nice. They helped me find my seat and get settled in with the baby. Francine had given me a pack of gum with instructions to start chewing before takeoff. I closed my eyes as we began taxing down the runway. My hands were sweating and my heart raced wildly. When the plane lifted off the ground, my stomach lurched and I was sure that I would be sick. I was sweating profusely by now and glad that the baby was asleep.

"Is this your first time on a plane," an older woman beside me asked gently.

I nodded, too afraid to speak.

"Start taking deep breaths that should help. And you may want to find something to focus on to keep your stomach from getting queasy."

I took her advice and tried to focus on the magazine in front of me. The plane lurched to the left and back to the right a few times before it finally leveled off. I couldn't bear to look out of the window, so I kept my eyes glued to the picture on the magazine.

"The worst of it is over, the lady whispered to me. While we're in the air, you will barely be able to tell that we're moving. It's almost like sitting at home in your living room."

I looked at her and smiled.

"Look, we're above the clouds. Have you ever seen such a majestic sight?"

I glanced out of the window and was immediately filled with amazement. I could hardly believe my eyes as we continued to soar in the sky.

I refused the peanuts and Coke that the stewardess offered me a few minutes later, not wanting anything to upset my stomach. It didn't take long for the uneasiness to pass, but it returned as soon as the captain announced that we needed to prepare for landing. My stomach began to protest again as the pilot began the rocky descent. The landing was worse than the takeoff and I was happy when the plane touched down.

Mama and Ms. Pearl were waiting to pick us up when we landed in North Charleston. It was hard to keep the tears from flowing when I saw them standing there. Mama hugged RJ so tight; he let out a howl in protest. It was good to see the two of them, but I wished Ms. Lucille could have been there too.

After collecting our bags, we made our way to Mama's house. I was glad that I had listened to Francine. I would still be on that bus dreading the hours that it would take to get home.

"That boy already been callin'," Mama said angrily.

"Chile, you know he ain't gonna let you go wid out a fight now that you got his son," Ms. Pearl added.

"Dee-Dee, you gonna have to think of what is best for you and that baby. It ain't gonna be easy. You know how he is."

"I know Mama," I said thoughtfully.

We drove the rest of the way in silence. I thought about the note that I left for Rodney on the pillow. He wasn't going to be happy about any of this, but he didn't have his family's best interest at heart. He wanted other women and me too and he couldn't have it both ways.

It didn't take long for us to unload the bags when we got to Mama's house. RJ had been a perfect little baby for most of the trip and he was beginning to get a little cranky.

Mama reached for him and tried to soothe him as I carried the bags upstairs to my old room. "Now, now little RJ, you had enough of all this and you 'bout ready to stay in one place right?" I heard her say as I trudged the suitcase up the steps.

"Lawd, I know that chile gonna be spoil now," Ms. Pearl said teasingly.

"I know I won't be the only one spoilin' him. You itchin' to get your hands on him right now."

"You sure right. It's my turn to hold him."

I laughed and shook my head at the two of them. As soon as I got in the room the phone rang. I knew it was Rodney and this time I was ready for him.

"Hello," I said, picking it up quickly before Mama could hang up on him.

"You didn't waste any time running back home did you?"

"No, I didn't," I answered.

"I hope you don't think you're going to take my son from me. I'm his father and he belongs with me."

He had obviously read my note. I was not ruffled.

"Were you thinking about our son when you were spending your time with Stephanie," I said evenly.

"You can talk tough now that you're there with your Mama, but it ain't over Dee-Dee and you are still my wife. You are not through with me."

"That's surprising Rodney. It seems you've been through with me for a while now."

"There was nothing going on between Stephanie and me. She was just a friend that's all."

"Oh, now she was just a friend. A couple weeks ago, you didn't even know who she was."

"I didn't tell you about her because I knew you were going to try to make a big deal out of nothing."

"For once in your life, tell the truth Rodney! You are a liar and you know it. You were messing around with her and I didn't have the proof before, but now I do."

"What proof? Big deal, I was in her car. That's all you got on me."

"You know what Rodney. I don't even care. Do you hear me? I do **not** care! I'm tired of you and tired of all of your lies!" I slammed the phone down and went back downstairs to get the rest of my bags. Mama and Ms. Pearl looked up at me.

"Don't let that boy get to you, Dee-Dee," Ms. Pearl said.

"That him on the phone?" Mama asked.

I nodded.

"You just gotta stand your ground," Ms. Pearl added.

I took the last bag upstairs and dropped it on the floor when the phone rang again. I sighed and snatched up the phone.

"Yes!"

"Dee-Dee, this is your mother-in-law. I'm callin' because I just talked to your husband and he said you left him and took the baby. How in the world can you leave your husband in a time like this," she asked angrily. "Your husband was just in an accident and his own wife wasn't there when he got home from the hospital."

I stood there listening as Mrs. Jackson went on and on about how I was not being a good wife to Rodney.

After I'd had enough, I interrupted her. "Yes, Mrs. Jackson, I did leave Rodney. I have had enough of him messing around on me and hitting me."

"Dee-Dee, the two of you were doing fine the last time I talked to you. You can't keep running home to your mother every time you and your husband have a little spat."

Mrs. Jackson was beginning to sound just like Rodney. "Your son choking me was more than a 'little spat'."

Mrs. Jackson went on as if she hadn't heard me. "Now why don't you go on back and take care of your husband. He needs you there to take care of him right now and that baby needs his father."

"Mrs. Jackson, I am sorry to disappoint you, but I am not going back to Rodney. I gave him a second chance and we ended up going through the same old mess. I'm not trying to keep him away from his son, but it is over between us."

"I hope you change your mind Dee-Dee. You know God hates divorce."

"I know Mrs. Jackson and I'm sure He hates adultery and for a man to mistreat his wife too."

Mrs. Jackson did not reply.

"I'm sorry Mrs. Jackson. I'm not trying to be disrespectful or anything, but I can't continue to live my life that way."

"When are we going to be able to see our grandson?"

"You are welcome to come over here to see him whenever you like. I don't want to keep him away from you."

"Please think about what you doing Dee-Dee."

"I will. Goodbye Mrs. Jackson." I hung up the phone and plopped down on the bed. *God please help me through this.* I sat there and thought about my predicament. I needed a job and fast. I had a son to take care of and with Rodney being so angry with me, a judge may have to force him to pay child support. That idea made me cringe. Men shouldn't have to be forced to take care of their children, but in this case, his rage may override him doing the right thing.

I went back downstairs to check on RJ. Ms. Pearl was holding him and trying desperately to get him to laugh.

"Was that him again," Mama asked worriedly.

"No. That was his mother this time."

I probably shouldn't have said that because as soon as the words came out of my mouth Mama and Ms. Pearl started in on her.

"What in the world she got to say?" Ms. Pearl demanded.

"She says I need to go back up there and take care of my husband."

"What! I shoulda known she would say that. That woman is out of her mind," Ms. Pearl declared.

"What do you expect? She only thinkin' bout her son. She ain't concerned about Dee-Dee." Mama balled her lips and shook her head.

The two women continued their discussion about Mrs. Jackson for the next fifteen minutes.

"You hungry Baby? I got some barbecue chicken and scalloped potatoes in there."

"I'm fine Mama."

"How your friend Francine doing? I'm so glad you had a friend like her."

"She's fine."

"I wish I could meet her and tell her thank you for how she helped you through all of this."

I nodded in agreement.

"You don't come by friends like that every day," said Ms. Pearl as she caressed RJ's chubby cheeks.

"Did you find out what happened to the girl he was in the car wid?"

"I asked Francine to let me know if she hears anything. She works there at the hospital."

"That's right. I remember you tellin' me that before."

"I hope her mama can make it from Korea to be there wid her."

I thought about the frail figure that I saw lying in the hospital bed. Even though she was the other woman, I felt sorry for her. It was not easy to resist Rodney. I couldn't remain angry with her or blame her for the breakup of my marriage. If it hadn't been her, it would have been someone else.

"I'm going to have to start looking for a job," I said not realizing that I was thinking out loud.

"Chile, you just got here and you thinkin' bout a job already."

"I have a son to take care of Mama. I don't want to be a burden on you."

"Now you know you not a burden on your mama," Ms. Pearl chided.

"I know, but soon I'll need to get my own place."

"Well, you already got a car. It's a good thing you didn't sell it."

"I don't want to take the car from the two of you. You'll need it."

Ms. Pearl and Mama exchanged glances and shook their head. "That car is yours. We don't drive it that much."

I looked at the two of them and knew that they had made their decision, so there was no point in discussing it further. "Just let me know when you need to go somewhere and I'll take you," I replied.

"We know that," Ms. Pearl said. "Dee-Dee this is one beautiful baby. I have to admit that he look just like his daddy though."

"He might look like him, but the most important thing is that he don't turn out like him," Mama said adamantly.

"Ain't that the truth," Ms. Pearl said agreeing with her.

I looked at my baby and knew that we had an uphill struggle ahead of us, but things would work out.

❧ Chapter 24 ❧

The harassing calls from Rodney continued in the weeks after I left Tennessee. His menacing words were always the same. He threatened me repeatedly and amazingly, they did not seem to have the same effect on me as before. Somehow he must have sensed that his threats were ineffective because he seemed more desperate in his attempts to get me to come back. I could tell that he was also drinking more heavily because his words were often slurred and he kept repeating the same phrases over and over.

One day when he called, I asked him about Stephanie. He refused to talk about her with me. "I called to talk about me and you," he replied forcefully. "I want to see my son!"

"Now is not a good time Rodney," I replied calmly.

"Well when is it a good time? It's been over a month."

"And whose fault is that," I asked.

"What do you mean whose fault is that? You took him from me. You are not going to keep me from my son."

"I'm not trying to keep him from you Rodney."

"As soon as I can travel, I am coming to get him. You can count on it," he threatened.

I tried to keep all of these things from Mama and only told her what I thought was necessary. The last call that I got from Rodney was the worst. His ranting went on and on until I finally decided to put the phone's headset under a pile of blankets before going to sleep. There was no point in hanging up on him because he called back every time and I needed to get my rest.

The manager at Woolworth's had given me my old job back, this time as a full time employee. I was thankful that Sharon was there to put in a good word for me. It didn't take long for me to fall back into the routine.

Sharon was ecstatic when she found out that I had been rehired. "Claudette, you need to come over for a visit so that I can see the baby, and I want you to see my new apartment."

"OK," I replied, "We need to find the right time though. Both of us are working crazy hours."

"I know girl, but we'll have to get together soon."

The day came when I finally had time to take her up on her offer. We agreed that I would come over one Friday afternoon since I was only working a half shift and she was getting off at four. Her apartment was fifteen minutes away from Mama's house. I drove around the block twice before I found the right one.

Sharon squealed with delight as soon as she opened the door. She immediately reached for RJ. "Claudette he is adorable. Just look at those little chubby cheeks."

I smiled as I watched her with the baby. She proceeded to fill me in on everything that had happened at the store since I left. I congratulated her on her promotion as supervisor over the jewelry department.

"Things really seem to be looking up for you now."

"I know. I can hardly believe it myself. I hated dropping out of school, but I couldn't pass up the offer when they offered me the position. My salary wasn't enough to take care of my son the way I needed to."

"I'm surprised that you decided to get your own place."

Sharon opened her eyes wide as she looked at me. "Why are you surprised? Girl, my mother was driving me crazy. She means well, but she was trying to control every aspect of my life."

We both laughed. "My mother isn't that way, but I would like to get a place of my own one day."

Sharon paused and then her face brightened. "Why don't we become roommates? I have two bedrooms."

I thought about the idea and promised to think about it.

"Travis' father isn't helping you take care of him at all?" I asked.

"Please, there is no point in wasting my time with him. He only seems to be interested in getting in my bed and that is not going to happen. I'm through messing around with married men. He got what he wanted and left me with a son to raise on my own."

Even though Sharon said it in a joking way, it was clear that she was still bitter about the experience. I don't know what made me want to open up to her about Rodney, but I did.

"I'm so sorry Claudette. You know what's weird? Listening to you, makes me realize how selfish I was in sleeping with that woman's husband. Her feelings didn't matter to me. I was only thinking about what I wanted and I allowed him to fill my head with a bunch of lies. He's the only one who got the prize in that game. If my mother hadn't talked some sense into me, he would still be running those games on me."

We were silent as we thought about our situations. I took that opportunity to look around the tiny apartment. She had done a good job of decorating it and making it look nice.

Sharon saw me looking around and smiled. "It's a good thing we work at Woolworth's huh? A lot of these things were purchased from there."

"Yes, it looks nice."

"Do you want something to drink?"

"I'll take some water if you don't mind. When I went for my last checkup, the doctor told me I needed to start drinking more water."

Sharon laughed. "Yeah, I need to do the same thing, but I hate water." She got up and went to the refrigerator.

"So who keeps Travis for you during the day?"

"My neighbor keeps him for me. My mother just couldn't do it anymore. They increased her hours on her job and she needed the money."

"Does she charge a lot?"

"No. She's pretty reasonable. She only charges me thirty dollars a week."

"Oh, that's not bad."

"Why? Do you need a sitter?"

"I'm just thinking about the possibilities if I move in. My mother has some health issues that could make it hard for her to watch RJ once he starts walking."

"Well, let me know if you want me to ask her for you. I'm sure she wouldn't mind. She's very good with Travis." Sharon looked at her watch. "It's almost time for me to go and get him. That's the other good thing about her being so close. I come home and put things away and pull myself together before I go to get him. As long as I'm there by six o'clock, she doesn't make a fuss about it. Do you want to come and meet her?"

"No. Not today. I'll do it another time." I was hesitant about committing to this before deciding whether or not I wanted to be Sharon's roommate. "I need to be getting home anyway. Thanks for inviting me over."

"You don't have to leave. I'll be right back."

"I really need to go. I have a lot of things to get done."

"Alright, I'm glad you were able to stop by. And let me know if you want to move in. The rent's not that bad."

"I'll let you know."

I gathered RJ's things and moved to the door. Sharon walked out with us and waited until I got him settled in the car. She waved before turning toward an apartment building across the street.

When I got back to Mama's house, I got out of the car and walked around to the passenger side to get RJ. I felt a presence behind me as soon as I scooped him up in my arms. When I stood up, Rodney was standing in front of me with a wild look on his face.

I was speechless.

He moved closer toward me. He reeked of alcohol. "Surprised to see me?"

For some strange reason, I looked at the house and prayed that Mama would come outside. Something was terribly wrong. I pulled RJ toward me and backed away. "What are you doing here?"

"I told you before that if I can't have you, no one else will."

"My body was shaking as I continued backing away from this stranger that I had once called my husband. The look in his eyes sent chills down my spine. "Mama's in the house and she's going to be coming out here in a minute," I said fearfully.

"In that case, I better take this out now, then."

He pulled out a small handgun and pointed it directly at my chest. I could not speak or move and I couldn't think clearly enough to pray. I heard a loud pop, but never felt the bullet that raced toward my chest. I fell backwards and hit the ground. I could hear RJ screaming as he lay on top of me. I gazed up in disbelief at the man who had promised to love me as he pointed the gun at my head.

After what seemed like an eternity, I heard my mother's high pitched voice as she yelled out, "What's going on here?"

Rodney shoved the gun in his pocket and ran behind the house.

"My God, Dee-Dee, are you alright?" Mama made her way down the steps as quickly as she could.

I tried to get up, but I couldn't move my right arm.

Mama stood over me and screamed.

"Get RJ, Mama," I whispered to her.

She quickly grabbed the baby and turned to go back in the house. "You stay there. I'm going to call 911."

I managed to lift myself up slowly and stood up beside the car.

"Help is on the way. Don't you worry." I turned to see an old woman standing behind me with the kindest eyes. "You know what you must do now don't you?"

Her question puzzled me and I didn't know how to respond.

She looked at me carefully and repeated the question. Before I could answer, Mama came rushing back outside. I heard Ms. Pearl calling my name as she ran toward us. Everything from that point on seemed very hazy.

"Can you walk," Mama asked as she ushered me toward the steps.

I didn't understand why she would ask me that question. Why would I not be able to walk? *What is wrong with my right arm*, I wondered. Why wasn't it moving like I wanted it to?

"Oh, my God," Ms. Pearl said when she reached me.

The two women helped me up the steps and took me into the house. "You lay down on that couch 'til the ambulance gets here," Mama said. She was crying and shaking like a leaf.

What do we need an ambulance for?"

Mama gave me the strangest look. "Baby, you've been shot!"

Her words took awhile to register in my mind. "The baby…"

"He's fine," Mama assured me. "He wasn't hit."

"Who was that old lady Mama?"

"What old lady?" She looked at me and frowned.

I told her about the old lady who had approached me and tried to describe her. Mama looked at me and frowned. "I don't know 'bout no old lady. You just rest until the ambulance gets here. Lawd Pearl, that no good boy shot my chile."

Ms. Pearl was fighting back tears as she caressed my arm. "She gonna be alright Hattie."

A few minutes later, we heard a knock at the door. Ms. Pearl ran to the door and peeked out of the peep hole. "It's the cops Hattie." She pulled the door open quickly.

Two officers walked into the house and came to stand beside me. "How you doing ma'am," one of them said as he looked down at me.

I kept wondering why I didn't feel anything. "I'm fine."

He kneeled down beside me to get a good look at the area that Mama and Ms. Pearl kept staring at.

"Ma'am your mother reported that your husband shot you. Is that correct?"

I nodded.

"We need you to give us a description of him and tell us what he was wearing."

I gave them the information they wanted. Mama ran over to the curio cabinet and grabbed our wedding picture. "Here's a picture."

The other officer took the picture from her and immediately pulled out his radio to call in the information. As soon as he started talking, we heard the blaring sound of the ambulance.

"Thank God they finally here," Mama whispered. Pearl get the baby and you drive Dee-Dee's car. I'm going in the ambulance with her."

Minutes later, several men in white uniforms ran into the house and started poking around my chest. It didn't take long for them to get me into the ambulance. It all seemed so surreal. The men around me began hooking me up to machines and talking to each other in codes that made no sense to me. Mama stayed right beside me and would not let go of my hand.

"Everything gonna be alright Dee-Dee."

It didn't take long for us to get to the hospital. I was quickly whisked into a room with a huge light that beamed directly in my face. I turned my head to the side in order to see what was going on around me. I was hooked up to additional machines as a nurse cut away my clothes. She got a large cotton ball and started dabbing in an area near my chest. I still couldn't feel anything.

A large, burly man with hazel eyes came over to examine me. "What's your name," he asked before pressing on the area near my shoulder.

Before I could tell him he yelled out to those standing around him. "I can see it. The clavicle is holding it."

His words were confusing to me, but I didn't bother to say anything. I felt the prick of a needle and the rush of a cold liquid coursing through my body.

"You're a lucky young woman, he said looking directly at me. The bullet is lodged in your clavicle, that's this big shoulder bone right here. As a result, you now have a broken collarbone." He touched the left side of my body so that I would know what he was talking about. "If that bone hadn't caught that bullet, it could have dropped down into your lungs. You're a very lucky young woman."

He took a pair of what looked like pliers and began tugging at something. A few minutes later, he held up a flattened piece of silver metal and showed it to me.

"This is the bullet. It's smashed, but it's in tact."

That's the last thing I remembered before everything went black.

I awoke a few hours later to excruciating pain. The upper right side of my body was wrapped tightly and a sling kept my arm pinned to my side. I groaned as I tried to move my body in the bed. Mama came to stand beside me as soon as she saw me moving around.

"How you feelin' Baby?" The sadness in her eyes was unbearable.

"I'm fine Mama. How's RJ?"

"He's alright. Don't worry 'bout him none. I told Pearl to take him back home. I'm stayin' wid you tonight. She'll be back in the mornin'."

"Mama are you sure? I'll be alright here. You don't have to stay here all night."

"I'm stayin' right here. Pearl is stayin' at my house and she'll be by here in the mornin' to get me."

I smiled weakly as I thought of Ms. Pearl having to get up in the middle of the night with RJ.

Suddenly Mama looked at me and started to cry. "They got him Dee-Dee. He was hidin' in the marshes behind the house, but the cops got 'em."

Mama held my hand tightly.

"I'm sorry to keep putting you through this Mama," I said miserably.

"Now you hush up 'bout that. I'm just thankful to God for lettin' you live. That boy coulda killed you Dee-Dee."

"I know."

"That ain't all Baby."

"The look in Mama's eyes made me shiver."

"What is it Mama?"

She shook her head sadly. He tried to fight one of the cops." Mama stopped as the tears flowed down her cheeks.

My heart raced wildly as I waited for her to go on. "What happened? Tell me," I pleaded.

"He tried to run away and they shot him. He didn't make it Baby."

"Oh my God!" I cried.

Mama held my hand gently as the tears began to flow. *This couldn't be happening.*

"I'm sorry Baby," Mama repeated over and over.

"I didn't want him to die," I wailed.

"I know that Dee-Dee. None of us expected it to end like this."

The nurse came in quietly. "Would you like me to prepare a sedative for her," she asked Mama.

The pain that I was feeling was unbearable and it would take a lot more than a sedative to make it go away. "Why?" I asked Mama. "Why did it have to end this way?"

"I know it hurts Baby. You just let it out."

The last thing I remembered was her patting my head softly and telling me that everything was going to be OK.

When I awoke hours later, I didn't realize that Mama was still in the room until she came over and rubbed my arm gently. "It's a shame it had to come to this, but things could have been worse," she said sadly.

"What exactly happened when they caught him?"

"The officer just left here. I didn't want to disturb you. He said Rodney denied it and told them your boyfriend did it. When they tried to put the handcuffs on 'em, he started fightin' and hit one of the officers before he got up and tried to run away. They told him several times to stop, but he kept going."

I could not believe what I was hearing. "He said what?"

Mama shook her head. "He denied it all and said he didn't do it."

"He had to be out of his mind."

"I don't doubt it. But according to that officer, the Army had reported him AWOL, whatever that means."

"That means that he was absent without leave. He obviously didn't show up for work and they couldn't get in touch with him."

"Lawd, chile, I'm sorry it had to end this way for you, but…" Mama stopped and wiped her eyes as the tears trickled down.

"I can't blame it all on him Mama. I married him for all the wrong reasons. I didn't know who I was when I met him."

Mama nodded sadly.

"Have you heard anything from his family?"

"Not his mama and daddy, but the nurse say his sister call here not long ago to check on you. That was nice of her."

"God, why did this have to happen?" I was still in shock and it was hard to believe that Rodney was gone.

Mama patted my arm again. "I been there myself so I know it's hard but you can make it through this. You got somebody dependin' on you now."

In my grief I had completely forgotten about RJ. My heart ached as I thought about him no longer having a father. "Did Ms. Pearl call to say how he's doing," I asked sadly.

"He doin' fine. It's a good thing you pumped all that extra milk this mornin', cause she say he been eatin' up a storm."

Mama, what am I going to do?" I moaned.

"Baby, you do what the rest of us do when we have to face somethin' like this? You trust God to see you through," she said firmly.

Long after Mama nodded off on the little cot the nurse had made ready for her in a corner of the room, I lay awake crying softly. She had ignored my many pleas to call a cab and go home.

As the tears ran crookedly down my face, I relived the last moments of my time with Rodney. My attention was drawn to Mama as she stirred on the narrow bed before going back to sleep. I closed my eyes tightly and prayed, *God help me to be as good a mother to my son as my mother has been to me. And please fix it so that she won't have to cry anymore tears of sorrow for me — only tears of joy.*

Discussion Questions for Single Individuals

1. What questions should you ask before entering into a relationship?

2. What should you know about the family/friends of the person you plan to marry?

3. How long is long enough to get to know someone before you enter into marriage?

4. How important is it to you for your family/friends to approve of the person you plan to marry?

5. What is your strategy to end a bad relationship before it gets too serious?

6. How will you know when you find your soul-mate? List five qualities that your soul-mate **must** have.

7. If your parents did not have the ideal relationship, what will you do to keep from making the same mistakes?

Discussion Questions for Married Individuals

1. What is your definition of being "happily' married"?

2. Does your mate believe that he/she is the most important person in your life? How do you know?

3. Is it acceptable to keep secrets from your mate? Why or why not?

4. List five of your mate's best qualities.

5. Would your children say that you are happily married?

6. In what ways can you make your relationship better?

7. Do you tend to affirm or criticize your mate?

About the Author...

As a teenager, Lorraine remembers hurrying to the mailbox to collect the next package of all newly arrived books. Out of this love for reading, grew the desire to write novels and short stories. She has written three books and is the coauthor of two plays. Lorraine uses her God-given gifts and talents to enlighten others about the importance of knowing who they are and encourages them to move toward their destiny.

Lorraine is a teacher, inspirational speaker and founder of Destiny's Daughters of Promise—a mentoring and leadership program for young women. She has earned a Master's degree in Education and is certified in Supervision and Administration. Lorraine is also a veteran of the United States Army (August 1981-March 1991) and recipient of the Meritorious Service Medal. Some of her military tours include assignments at Fort Campbell and Ft. Knox, Kentucky, with overseas tours in Ansbach and Wuerzburg, Germany.

Lorraine resides in Kennesaw, GA with her husband, Charles a retired veteran and recipient of the Bronze Star Medal. She is the mother of two adult children and grandmother of one. Lorraine continues to seek ways to perfect her talents in ways that will captivate and challenge the reader with the truth of God's word.

Lorraine is a member of Word of Faith Family Worship Cathedral in Austell, Georgia where she is actively involved in the Christian Education Department. **Connect with Lorraine at:**

Website: www.hiswordinseason.com
Blog: blog.hiswordinseason.com
Email: lorrainethomas@hiswordinseason.com

Other Books by this Author

Unequally Yoked
ISBN:0-9767828-7-1
$12.95

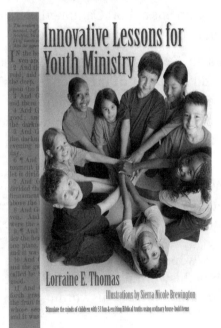

Innovative Lessons for Youth Ministry
ISBN:13: 978-0-9777060-9-9
$14.00

Quick Order Form

Postal Orders: His Word In Season, PO Box 801479,
Acworth, GA 30101

Please send the following book(s).

(Quantity)

_____   *Unequally Yoked ($12.95)*

_____   *A Promise to Love ($14.95)*

_____   *Innovative Lessons for Youth Ministry ($14.00)*

Order online at : www.hiswordinseason.com

Name:_____

Address:_____

_____

City:_____State:_____Zip:_____

E-mail address:_____

Include check or money order for the items ordered plus
$4.95 SH. Please add an additional $1.00(ea.) for quantities of 3 or more.

*Sales Tax: Add 6% for items mailed to an address in Georgia.

____ Please add my name to your mailing list for updates about future
      items.